"Ryan, I don't want you to die for me."

Jessica had followed his orders all day and had the blisters to prove it. She wasn't putting up with any more today. She jabbed her finger against his chest. "Four marshals died protecting me. I don't want your name branded into my conscience, too."

She whirled around and stomped through the bushes, struggling to hold back the angry words she wanted to say. For the first time since she'd testified, she'd gone on the offensive, determined to protect Ryan in any way she could. For what? So he could lecture her?

"Jessie, wait."

Ryan caught up to her and grasped her shoulders. He forced her to turn around, but she refused to look up at him.

"When I couldn't find you, I thought someone had…" His words faded away and he pulled her tightly against his chest.

He was worried about her? That's why he was so angry?

He gently pushed Jessica back and cupped her face between his hands. "Don't *ever* scare me like that again."

Ryan yanked her toward him and captured her lips in a fierce kiss….

LENA DIAZ

THE MARSHAL'S WITNESS

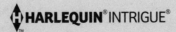

Thank you Allison Lyons for loving my story. Thank you Nalini Akolekar for seeing the Harlequin Intrigue author inside me before I did. This book is dedicated to my *special* sister, Laura Brown, for fighting the good fight against breast cancer, and for being the inspiration for me to chase my dreams. I love you.

ISBN-13: 978-0-373-74726-9

THE MARSHAL'S WITNESS

Copyright © 2013 by Lena Diaz

Recycling programs for this product may not exist in your area.

HARLEQUIN®
www.Harlequin.com

Printed in U.S.A.

ABOUT THE AUTHOR

Lena Diaz was born in Kentucky and has also lived in California, Louisiana and Florida where she now resides with her husband and two children. Before becoming a romance suspense author, she was a computer programmer. A former Romance Writers of America Golden Heart® finalist, she won the prestigious Daphne du Maurier award for excellence in mystery and suspense. She loves to watch action movies, garden and hike in the beautiful Tennessee Smoky Mountains. To get the latest news about Lena, please visit her website, www.lenadiaz.com.

Books by Lena Diaz

HARLEQUIN INTRIGUE
1405—THE MARSHAL'S WITNESS

CAST OF CHARACTERS

Ryan Jackson—This U.S. Marshal must use every ounce of his survival skills as a former army ranger to try to keep his witness alive, even though her criminal past offends his deep sense of honor and justice.

Jessica Delaney—After testifying against her boss, this former mob accountant goes into the Witness Protection Program. But her new life is nearly cut short by an assassin and she must go on the run with her U.S. Marshal protector.

Richard DeGaullo—This crime lord wants Jessica Delaney dead, but is he the one behind the leak in Witness Protection? Or is someone else trying to kill his former accountant?

Alex Trask—Is Ryan's boss really trying to help Ryan get Jessica to safety? Or is he the one who leaked her location?

Stuart Lanier—This private investigator is one of Ryan's closest friends and served with him in the army. He's one of the few people Ryan trusts completely. But is that trust deserved?

Alan Rivers—Deputy director of the CIA. He works closely with the director, but he may be working even more closely with someone else.

Dominic Ward—Director of the CIA. When Ryan was in the army, Dominic worked with Ryan's commanding officer to provide intelligence for special ops missions.

Chapter One

One juror. That's all it had taken to set a murderer free.

Jessica Delaney flattened her hands against the conference-room window of the White Plains Federal courthouse, watching the mockery playing out two stories below.

Mistrial. The word left a bitter taste in her mouth. What would that juror have done if *his* friend had been brutally murdered in front of him? Or if his life had become the nightmare Jessica's had become, living in fear that her former boss would discover where the government was keeping her during the year-long trial?

She'd been foolish to think her testimony could make a difference, that a twenty-eight year-old accountant could put the head of the most powerful crime family in New York away, when others had tried and failed before her. She'd given up everything—her home, her friends, her job—to become the government's star witness. For what? DeGaullo was free, and she was about to go into hiding.

For the rest of her life.

Her hands tightened into fists as Richard De-Gaullo waded through the crowd of reporters, smiling and waving like a foreign dignitary instead of a man who'd viciously executed a young mother, leaving two small children behind to mourn her death.

He jogged down the steps, his perfectly pressed suit jacket flapping in the wind as the first fat raindrops from an afternoon storm splattered against Jessica's window. Freedom waited for DeGaullo in the form of a black stretch limo snugged up against the curb.

The driver opened the rear door. Jessica sucked in her breath when DeGaullo turned and looked up, as if he knew she was watching. He raised his hand in a jaunty salute, flashed a cocky grin, then slid inside the car.

A loud knock sounded behind Jessica, making her start in surprise. She turned around to see a man she didn't know, standing in the open doorway. The briefcase he held looked like a child's toy in his large hand, and the top of his head barely cleared the door frame.

Jessica's gaze darted past him to the marshals in the hallway. William Gavin, the marshal who led her security detail, gave her a reassuring nod before closing the door, cocooning her in with the stranger.

A polite greeting died on Jessica's lips as the

man strode toward her, his angular face tightening into lines of disapproval. With his coal-black suit emphasizing his massive shoulders, he looked like an avenging angel, or a demon, swooping down to punish her for her sins. She tensed against the urge to flinch away when he stopped in front of her.

"Move away from the window." He gently but firmly pushed her away from the glass. The look in his dark blue eyes, as he scanned the courtyard below, reminded her of a hawk sighting its prey. Seemingly satisfied, he flipped the blinds closed and crossed the tiny room to the table in the corner.

He pulled out a chair and raised an expectant brow. Jessica reluctantly obeyed his unspoken command, taking the seat he offered. She stiffened when he leaned down, his lips next to her ear.

"Never stand in front of a window, especially with the light behind you," he said. "Don't make it easy for him."

She shivered at the feel of his warm breath whispering across her skin, and the deadly warning in his words—words that rang true after seeing De-Gaullo wave at her. Since the stranger seemed to be waiting for a response, she nodded.

He moved to the chair across from her and set his briefcase on the table.

"I was told the glass is bulletproof." Jessica immediately regretted her statement when she realized how defensive she sounded.

The stranger's dark brows arched but he didn't

bother to look at her. He was more concerned with the papers in his briefcase.

Jessica pressed her lips together and took the opportunity to study him. Tiny lines bracketed his mouth. On someone else they would have been laugh lines, but she couldn't picture this man laughing. His eyes were guarded, as if he'd seen too much, and the tragedies in his life had stamped themselves onto his soul.

He took three pieces of paper out of his briefcase and placed them on the table in front of her. "Nothing's bulletproof if you have the right weapon, the right motivation." His deep voice echoed through the small space. "Your former boss has plenty of both." He reached a tanned hand into his suit jacket, pulled out a pen, and tossed it across the table.

Jessica managed to snatch the pen before it could fall onto the floor. "Who *are* you?" She slapped the pen down on the table.

"Deputy U.S. Marshal Ryan Jackson."

Jessica's face flushed as she recognized the arrogant disdain on his stern features. He didn't approve of her, and he didn't try to hide it. Jessica curled her fists in her lap. She was so sick of being judged by people who didn't even know her. The last year had been a trial in more ways than one, sitting in the courtroom every day, feeling the weight of the jurors' stares, their contempt.

As if her *own* guilt wasn't enough.

She leaned forward and waved her hand at the papers. "What's all this?"

"Official acknowledgement of the WitSec rules before you take on your new identity."

"WitSec?"

"Witness Security."

"Marshal Cole always calls it Witness Protection," she murmured absently as she skimmed the pages. "Why isn't he here to take care of this? He's the one I usually work with when there's any paperwork to be done."

"He's unavailable." Without giving her a chance to ask any more questions, Ryan pointed to one of the pages. "This is your acknowledgement of the first rule of the program. Never contact anyone from your previous life. No snail mail, email, text messages and especially no phone calls."

"I know the rules." She scrawled her signature beneath the statement.

"Rule number two," he said, as if she hadn't spoken, "never go anywhere you've ever lived or even visited in the past. Five, ten years from now, you still can't go back. Ever."

Hearing those words in Ryan Jackson's ominous tone made the second rule sound even worse than she'd remembered. This was the last time she'd ever see the beloved city where she'd spent most of her adult life.

Who would have thought she'd miss the smell of exhaust as the rows of taxi cabs jostled for position every morning, or the constant flood of tourists getting in her way on the sidewalk? She would definitely miss the aroma of fresh-baked bread wafting out of cafés, and the thick, juicy cheeseburgers at Junior's, with cheesecake for dessert—plain, the way it was supposed to be.

After today, nothing would ever be the same again.

Her hand shook as she signed on the dotted line. Ryan's gaze flicked up to her face.

Jessica blinked, fighting back an unexpected rush of tears. She wasn't about to cry in front of a stranger, especially a stranger as cold as the one across from her.

He watched her intently as he recited the last rule. "Never tell anyone about your past. Break any of these rules and the government can toss you out of the program. More importantly, break any of these rules and your life *will* be in danger. No one has ever been killed in WitSec, as long as they followed these three rules."

His dark eyes narrowed at her. "People who break these rules die. Do you understand?"

Her stomach did a little flip and a deep sense of dread crept over her. The fear that always simmered beneath the surface threatened to take hold. But with Ryan watching her so closely, as if he expected her to break down at any moment, she straightened her shoulders and tried not to let him see how much his words had affected her.

"I understood the rules the first five times I heard

them." She signed the last page with a flourish and raised a brow. "Are we done?"

She tossed the pen across the table, forcing him to grab it before it fell on the floor.

The corner of his mouth tilted up in a grin, surprising her. "Not quite."

He shoved the pen and papers into the briefcase, his expression sobering, as if he realized he'd let his guard down. "You've memorized your new identity?"

"Marshal Cole has grilled me for months to prepare me. I'm not likely to forget."

"Convince me. What's your name?"

She tapped her foot, irritated that she had to go through the same routine again. "Jessica Adams."

"Address?"

"New Orleans, Louisiana."

He raised a brow.

She blew out a frustrated breath and rattled off the address—a house number and a street that meant nothing to her, but that were more ingrained in her memory now than her real New York City address had ever been.

He fired off questions about her fake bio, her new social security number, the names and birthdates of her pretend family. For the first time in her life, she was grateful that the foster families who'd shuffled her back and forth had always kept her at a distance, as if they were afraid her bad genes were contagious. If she'd had a real family, people who loved her and were loved in return, she didn't think she could give them up and leave them behind.

Ryan shoved back from the table and rose to his feet. "Ready?"

Was she ready? Ready to move a thousand miles away to a place she'd never been, a place she'd never wanted to be? Was she ready to have her past erased as if she'd never existed, living in fear that Richard DeGaullo would find her and punish her for betraying him?

Her stomach twisted into knots. She wanted to cling to her chair and hide, but that wasn't an option. All she could do now was face her future, however uncertain it might be.

"I'm ready." She stood and wiped her sweaty palms on her slacks, and followed him to the door.

He paused with his hand on the knob, his mouth curving up into the first genuine smile he'd shown since entering the room. "You're going to be okay, Jessica Adams."

And with that, he was gone, striding down the hallway, leaving her with her usual contingent of marshals.

"Ready, Jessica?" William echoed Ryan's earlier words.

She tore her gaze away from Ryan's retreating back, stunned by how his smile had completely transformed his features, giving her a glimpse of the lighthearted man he must have once been. She cleared her tightening throat. "Ready."

The four marshals flanked her on all sides as they headed down the hallway toward the back stairs. One of the marshals moved to let another man pass and gave him a curt nod. Jessica frowned, surprised the marshal had let the stranger get so close to her. He must have been someone the marshal knew and trusted.

Thoughts of the stranger evaporated as Jessica descended the stairs, getting closer and closer to the bottom. By the time her feet touched the last step, her instincts were screaming at her to run, hide—anything but walk toward the exit at the end of the hall.

Her heart pounded in rhythm with her steps. Twenty feet to the door.

Nineteen.

Eighteen.

Too fast. Slow down. Please, slow down.

Far too soon they stood at the back door. Had she said she was ready? She was wrong. She *wasn't* ready.

Her pulse leaped in her throat. Soon she'd be completely, utterly alone, without marshals guarding her twenty-four-seven. Her safety would depend on a web of lies and documentation, her fate in the hands of some paper pusher she'd never met.

Panic tightened her chest. She jumped when one of the marshals opened the door and it slammed against the wall, caught by a blast of surprisingly chilly wind for early September. The oak trees lining the street swayed, their branches clicking together like tiny drummers foretelling her doom.

With William urging her forward, she had no choice but to move. She couldn't cling to the door and cower in fear.

She stepped outside.

A gust of wind and rain blasted her, whipping her hair around her face. The light sprinkle that had started earlier was now a steady downpour, pelting the small group as they hurried across the concrete to the street that ran along the back of the courthouse. A black cargo van waited fifty feet away at the curb. Uniformed policemen lined the sidewalk.

Thunder cracked overhead, making Jessica jump. Lightning flashed, filling the air with the smell of something burning, reminding Jessica of gunfire the night her friend was killed—the flash, the smell.

The spray of blood as Natalie fell to the floor, DeGaullo standing over her.

The van's open door was dark and menacing in the maelstrom of wind and rain. Jessica couldn't breathe. Her lungs squeezed in her chest. Was this how Natalie had felt as she died?

Please, I don't want to die.

Thunder boomed again and the rain became a deluge. Three of the marshals ran ahead to the van, positioning themselves to watch for anyone approaching. Jessica froze, unable to take another step. She was too exposed, too vulnerable, the safety of the van too far away.

"Come on," William urged. "We're almost there." He pushed her forward.

She stumbled, gasping for air.

Someone shouted, but the words were snatched away by the wind. Jessica whirled toward the sound. Ryan Jackson stood in the open courthouse doorway. He dropped his briefcase and sprinted toward her, his arms and legs pumping like an Olympic runner. He might have shouted her name, but she wasn't sure.

William cursed and grabbed her shoulders. Another shout, a metallic click, an explosion of light and sound. A wall of searing heat slammed into Jessica. She tumbled through the air, her screams mingling with the screams of others as the concrete rushed up to meet her. A sickening thud, burning, tearing agony, then…nothing.

Chapter Two

Smooth, soft sheets surrounded Jessica. But the fluffy pillow beneath her head did nothing to relieve the searing, throbbing pain that shot through her body. She tried to open her eyes, but her lids were too heavy, the pain too intense. The smell of antiseptic wafted through the air. A high-pitched beep sounded from far away.

Pain jackknifed through her head. She cried out, squeezing her eyes against the harsh light filtering through her lids. She tried to raise her hands to block out the light, but someone grabbed her arms, forcing them down.

"Let me go," she cried, but her dry throat made coherent speech impossible. The words sounded garbled even to her own ears.

"Hold her still before she hurts herself," a man's exasperated voice ordered.

"I'm trying, Doctor," said another male voice, inches from her face. "She's stronger than she looks."

"She's in pain." A woman's voice. "Can I give her the morphine now?"

Morphine? Jessica relaxed slightly against the hands holding her. Yes, morphine. *Please.* Everything hurt, especially her head.

"Not yet. I'm trying to wake her up, not put her back under."

Back under?

"Ms. Adams, I'm Dr. Brooks. You've been in an accident. Can you open your eyes?"

An accident? She gasped and cried out when the hands holding her down pressed on the upper part of her left arm.

"Be careful, David. You're pressing on her stitches." Dr. Brooks. The man who wouldn't give her morphine.

A stab of hot, sharp pain shot through the left side of Jessica's face. She moaned and tried to pull away from the rough, calloused hands holding her so tightly.

"Give her some morphine." The doctor, sounding impatient. "One-third the usual dose, just enough to calm her down."

"It's okay," a feminine voice whispered to Jessica. Soothing, gentle hands brushed against her. A low beep sounded. Moments later the pain dulled to a bearable ache and the urge to sleep flooded her veins. She fought its tempting pull and opened her eyes, blinking against the bright fluorescent lights.

A young man in lime-green scrubs was leaning over her bed, his hands clamping her wrists down.

"Release her, David," the voice she recognized as Dr. Brooks ordered.

The man in green let go of her arms and she pulled them against her chest. She turned her head on the pillow to put a face to the voice she'd heard. An unsmiling man stood on her right side. Instead of the white smock she'd expected, he wore an immaculate dark blue suit, his short, blond hair lightly curling around his face.

"Miss Adams, do you know where you are?" he asked.

She looked at the bed's metal railing, the IV pump, the stethoscope draped around the doctor's collar. "Hos…hospital," she rasped.

"That's right. Cohen Children's Medical Center."

Children's? That didn't make sense. Wait…wasn't that in Long Island? She was in Louisiana, wasn't she? She tried to speak again but her throat was too dry, too tight.

The doctor motioned to the older woman standing beside him, dressed in a Daisy Duck smock. "Get her some ice chips."

The woman left the room. The man in green adjusted the IV drip. When the woman returned, she held a yellow paper cup to Jessica's lips.

"Let these melt in your mouth, sweetie. I bet your throat's as dry as dust about now."

Jessica gratefully accepted the cool ice chips, instantly liking the short, rotund woman whose voice she recognized as the lady who'd wanted to give her morphine.

When her throat lost some of its dry, scratchy feel, she offered the nurse a weak smile. "Thank you."

The nurse patted her hand and motioned to the man the doctor had called David. They both left the room.

The doctor flashed a light in her eyes and listened to her heart. "Do you remember the explosion?"

Explosion? Oh, no. She squeezed her eyes tightly shut as horrific images assaulted her. The boom she'd thought was thunder, so loud her eardrums ached. The blast of heat. Burning, tearing pain as something ripped into her flesh. A sickening crack. A moment of intense agony when something hit her head with the force of a battering ram.

She gasped and opened her eyes. "I remember."

"Excellent." He didn't seem to notice her distress. "The headache you're experiencing is from a cracked skull. That was your most serious injury, but you've got enough stitches in you to sew a patchwork quilt. Minor burns, scrapes. You had a collapsed lung when you were taken to the ER. Your face—"

She tried to focus on his words, but in her mind's eye she saw Ryan Jackson back at the courthouse, running toward her, shouting her name. Why? What had he seen?

"—multiple contusions," the doctor continued. "I've kept you heavily sedated to control the swelling in your brain, but you're past the danger point now. I expect you'll make a complete recovery."

She twisted her fingers in the sheets, noticing for the first time that they were pink, covered with cartoon fairies and flowers. The walls were painted in soothing pastels. "Where am I?"

He sighed impatiently. "Cohen Children's Medical Center," he repeated, "in Long Island. Apparently some very bad people are after you. Your bodyguard transferred you here once you were stable. He seems to think that no one will look for you in a place like this."

"Long Island? Bodyguard?"

The doctor looked past her toward the other side of the room. "You have five minutes." With his crisp order lingering in the air, he strode out the doorway.

Bewildered by the doctor's abrupt departure, Jessica turned her head and met the icy stare of Marshal Ryan Jackson, sitting in a chair across the room.

Something about that look filled her with dread.

She recoiled against the sheets before she could stop herself. The mocking look on his face told her he'd noticed her reaction.

"You're as pleased to see me as I am to see you." His harsh voice raked across her nerve endings, making her head pound harder. He slowly unfolded his long, muscular body from the chair and crossed the short space to stand by her bed.

She could feel the heat from him, smell the light, clean scent of his soap. In another lifetime he would have been appealing. But her attraction to him was eclipsed by the anger rolling off him in waves.

She fought the urge to squirm farther away and concentrated on asking what she desperately needed to know. "What happened? The other marshals, how badly were they hurt?"

His lips flattened. "All dead. The only reason you're alive is because you didn't get into that van, and because Marshal Gavin shielded you with his body."

She covered her mouth, swallowing hard against the bile rising in her throat. She'd spent nearly every waking minute with those marshals for twelve months. She knew what foods they liked, what shows they watched, what made them laugh or curse.

Her heart twisted painfully in her chest and she shook her head in denial. She immediately stilled when the throbbing in her head worsened. "What happened?" she whispered, gritting her teeth against the pain.

"Someone, presumably one of DeGaullo's men, blew up the van using a damn toy, a remote-control car. I saw the car a few seconds before the blast." His jaw tightened. "My warning came too late. Except for you. Ironic, isn't it? A woman who dedicated her life to cooking the books for the mob survives, while four decent, honorable men die."

She jerked back from the raw fury and accusation in his voice. The sudden movement caused a wave of nausea. She sucked in a deep breath and bit back the sharp retort hovering on her tongue. Ryan Jackson didn't know her, or why she'd made the choices she'd made. He'd just seen his colleagues die, and he obviously blamed her, at least partially. She could understand that. She'd probably feel the same way.

"When are the funerals?" She struggled for a calmness she was far from feeling. "I want to go."

"You can't go to their funerals." He spoke in short, clipped tones.

Anger flared inside her, overriding her sympathy for him, overriding her horror over what had happened. "I don't care what you think of me, but I have to go to their funerals. I owe them that."

He reached toward her arm. Before she could move away, he gently lifted her wrist and unwound the IV tubing that had become tangled around one of her bandages.

"Whether I would have allowed you to go to their funerals is a moot point. In spite of your *miraculous* survival, you didn't come away unscathed in the blast. You've already been here for quite some time, and the doctor said you'll be here several more weeks, maybe longer. The funerals were held a few days after the explosion."

She clasped her hands on the railing beside her,

hatred for DeGaullo filling her like a living thing. He'd hurt so many people, including the one person she'd opened up to about her past—Natalie—and now he'd stolen her right to pay her respects to the men who'd died protecting her. "How long has it been since the explosion?"

He pulled up her covers and arranged the call button so she could easily reach it. He tugged at the wrinkles in her blanket, smoothing them out.

She frowned at his actions. It dawned on her, from the faraway look in his eyes, and the way his expression had softened, that he probably didn't realize what he was doing. His movements seemed automatic, like he was operating on autopilot.

The lines around his eyes were deeper than before. He looked tired, almost haggard. Silver threads shone in his dark hair, as if he'd aged several years since she'd met him at the courthouse.

His hands stilled. He straightened, his eyes frosting over, his cold mask back in place. "Two weeks. The funerals were two weeks ago."

He yanked his hand back and crossed to the window. A moment later, he squared his shoulders and turned around to face her. "I'm the lead field agent on your case now. When you leave here, I'll take you to a new location, settle you into another new identity."

Her mouth dropped open and she stared at him. She shook her head in denial, no longer caring that it made the pain worse. "No. I won't agree to that. You're too angry. You obviously blame me for what happened. I'll tell the Justice Department that I won't—"

"You think I want to be assigned to this case?" His jaw went rigid as he stepped back to her side. "You're not an innocent bystander who happened to witness a crime. You *chose* to cover up your boss's crimes for five years. The only reason you went to the Feds was because DeGaullo killed your friend, and you knew you were next. As far as I'm concerned, you're almost as bad as he is."

Her body flushed hot beneath his scalding words.

"But," he continued, before she could speak, "since I'm a former army ranger, and people are trying to kill you, the government has decided I'm their most qualified marshal to keep you alive. Against my wishes, they've assigned me as your temporary guardian."

His eyes flashed as he held her gaze. "Four men gave their lives for you. I'm not going to allow their sacrifices to be meaningless. When I became a marshal, I made a vow that I'm honor bound to keep. I *will* keep you safe, whatever it takes, whether you want me to or not."

RYAN FIRMLY SHUT the door to Jessica's hospital room and slumped back against the wall in the hallway. He scrubbed his hands across his face and rubbed his tired eyes. For two weeks he'd sat in that uncomfortable plastic chair in the corner of Jessica's room, watching over her. He'd slept in the cramped window seat, listening to the machines hooked up to her beeping along with her vital signs, calling the nurses when she cried out in pain. He'd held her hand when she twisted against the sheets in the throes of a nightmare.

And the minute she woke up, he'd been a complete jerk, blaming her for his friends' deaths. Did he blame her? Yes, partly, but that didn't excuse his actions. His mother would be appalled if she'd seen her son treat a woman that way, any woman, regardless of what she'd done.

Especially since the reason he'd behaved that way had nothing to do with the explosion, and everything to do with the way she affected him. When he'd looked into her soft brown eyes and that shock of attraction rippled through him, just like when he'd first met her, he'd been so disgusted at himself that he'd lashed out. How could he want her so much, knowing about her past, the choices she'd made that went against everything he believed in?

Physically, she was exactly his type—petite and curvy. Even with her stitches and bandages, she made his blood run hot. He could understand that. She was a beautiful woman, and he was still young enough to appreciate that. What he couldn't understand was why her appeal went far beyond her outward appearance.

When he looked in her eyes he saw the pain she didn't acknowledge, the kind of pain that went far deeper than cuts and bruises. He knew what caused that pain in him—the lives he'd taken while performing his duties, the betrayal by someone he'd trusted, the men under his command who'd lost their lives as a result of that betrayal.

But why was *she* suffering? What had happened to put those shadows in her eyes?

And why did he care?

He rubbed his neck to work out the stiffness. He didn't know what it was about Jessica Delaney that drove him so crazy. All he knew for sure was that he needed to put some distance between the two of them. The only way to do that was to finalize her new identity and get her new location set up.

He reached into his jacket pocket, pulled out his cell phone, and texted the message that would set everything into motion…*Sleeping Beauty is awake.*

Chapter Three

In the three weeks since she'd awakened in the hospital to find Ryan Jackson in her room, Jessica had learned a few things. One was that he had a bit of the devil in him. So, as she stood beside him on the front lawn that had already turned brown in the cool fall air, she did everything she could to hide her disappointment. She didn't want to give him the satisfaction of knowing he'd won this round, because the house he'd brought her to was the ugliest she'd ever seen.

And it was hers.

She glanced over at the three marshals leaning against the SUV in the gravel driveway. Judging by the looks on their faces, they agreed with her.

The house boasted rotting wood siding in a sickly mustard-yellow with patches of gray, as if someone had thought about changing the color but had changed their mind. The shutters on the two narrow front windows were missing half their slats. Weeds grew wild and tall, choking what once must have been a concrete walkway that led to the sagging porch.

"I suppose you would have rather gone to New Orleans." Ryan studied the dilapidated cabin in front of them as if weighing its merits. "Probably more appealing to a *city girl* like you."

Jessica pursed her lips, determined not to let his latest *city girl* comment goad her. He flung the mantra around as if it were the worst insult he could think of. It made her want to ask him why he didn't consider himself a *city boy* since he lived in New York, but that would require an actual conversation, and he wasn't open to that—not about anything personal, anyway.

Her shoulders slumped. He was right. Living in the gator-filled bayous of Louisiana would have been infinitely preferable to living in rural Tennessee.

Emphasis on rural.

He'd scrapped the original location, reasoning that her notoriety after the bombing would put her at risk in a big city. She was more inclined to believe he just wanted to punish her, especially since her new last name so clearly demonstrated his opinion of her.

Benedict.

As in Benedict Arnold.

"You'll have plenty of privacy on this dead-end road." He sounded like a Realtor trying to convince his client a house was cozy instead of cramped.

She glanced over at the only other house close enough to see, a cabin next to hers with about thirty feet separating the two. Its yard was well kept. Its porch had a collection of bleached-white rocking chairs and terra-cotta pots with purple cold-weather flowers spilling over the edge.

In the twenty-minute ride up the mountain, bumping and jarring over every pothole and rock on the gravel road, Jessica had only seen a handful of other houses. What were the odds that whoever lived next door would be her age, someone with the same likes and dislikes, someone she could be friends with? Knowing that Ryan had helped his boss choose this location for her, she figured the odds were just about zero. Ryan wouldn't want to reward the woman he held responsible for his friends' deaths.

"Who lives in the cabin next door?" she asked, bracing herself for the worst.

"Me."

"What?" Her mouth dropped open in shock. When she'd braced herself for the worst, having Ryan living next door wasn't even on the list of possibilities.

He opened the neon blue front door and rolled her suitcase inside. "For the next few weeks, I'll be your neighbor. Just until you're settled in."

"Oh, sugar."

The corner of Ryan's mouth lifted into a grin. "What did you say?"

"Nothing." Jessica wasn't about to admit that she'd grown up swearing worse than most boys, and that her last foster mom had gone on a personal crusade to clean up Jessica's language. She'd made Jessica say *sugar* instead of cussing, a habit that had become so ingrained, it had stuck with her. Ryan would jump all over that and tease her mercilessly.

She brushed past him through the foyer into the main room. When she saw the faded, baby blue sectional, the dark wood paneled walls, and orange shag carpet, she had to clamp her mouth shut to keep from saying sugar.

Or something worse.

Ryan joined her, his mouth twitching as he looked around.

Jessica curled her fingers into her palms and kept her face carefully blank.

"Nice fireplace," Ryan said, not bothering to hide his grin.

Jessica raised her brow at the behemoth sitting in the corner of the room. Big. That's the only word that came to mind when she stared at the soot-covered stonework that went from floor to ceiling. Okay, ugly came to mind, too, but that pretty much applied to the entire house.

Fighting back her despair, she followed Ryan to the left side of the house that contained two small bedrooms separated by a bathroom.

The bathroom was tiny but clean, with a soft peach color on the walls. She'd have to replace the shower curtain because the colors didn't match anything else in the room, but other than that… wait, what was on the shower curtain? What she'd thought were little birdhouses, on closer inspection were *outhouses,* with red and blue cartoon cats crawling all over them.

Her gaze flew to Ryan's. He returned her stare, silently daring her to complain, confirming her suspicion without saying a word. She didn't know how he'd managed it, but somehow he was responsible for that hideous shower curtain. She wouldn't put it past him to have ordered the thing online.

Beyond annoyed, she tried to shove past him to get out of the room, but all she managed to do was wedge herself against him in the doorway.

"Would you please move?" she said, her face flushing hot.

His brows raised and his eyes flicked down to where her breasts were crushed against him. She expected him to make some kind of rude comment, but instead he jerked to the side, breaking the contact between them and leaving the doorway clear. His mouth clamped shut as he stared at the oval mirror above the sink, waiting for her to leave.

She rushed from the tiny room, desperate to put some distance between her and Ryan. If he'd been any other man she would understand why her pulse was racing and her breasts were tingling after touching him. But this was *Ryan,* a man who despised her. How could she possibly respond to him that way?

What made her humiliation worse was the way he'd reacted. How could her traitorous body yearn for his touch when he was so disgusted by her that he couldn't even look at her?

He caught up to her and silently led the way back to the front of the house to the garage. He opened the door, just off the foyer, revealing a wall of boxes that contained all of her belongings, and a white compact the government had leased for her. Neither of them spoke. She self-consciously fingered her shoulder-length hair, newly shortened as a concession to her new identity.

The tour ended at a round, café-style table in the right, back corner of the living room just off the end of the kitchen. Ryan placed his briefcase on the table and clicked it open.

Jessica was too numb to even react when she noticed the rows of hideous red and yellow roosters marching across the wallpaper in the kitchen. All she cared about right now was getting through the next few minutes with some of her dignity intact, so she could be alone in her misery.

Ryan tossed a ring of keys on the table. He spread out a map, the crisp pages crinkling as he drew a red circle around a dot marked "Providence," the town they'd driven through at the bottom of the mountain.

He drew another circle a short distance away, and

connected the two circles with a red line. "This is your house," he said, pointing to one of the circles. "Take the road out front down the mountain to get to town. They have everything you need—a grocery store, gas station, hardware store. There's a diner across from the hardware store that I'm told serves a decent breakfast. There are a couple of chain restaurants farther down Main Street, and a handful of specialty shops."

He extended the red line past Providence, down the interstate and circled another black dot. "For serious shopping, take I-40 West to Sevierville."

"Sevierville?" She remembered passing through that city on the way here. "Isn't that about two hours away?"

"I did warn you this location was isolated."

Saying Providence was isolated was like comparing a hurricane to a light, summer breeze.

Jessica's shoulders slumped again. "When you described this place, I thought it would be like Gatlinburg, a tourist town with cabins clustered together all through the mountains. I didn't think I'd be so...alone up here." She stopped her nervous chatter, already dreading his next *city girl* comment.

The silence drew out and she glanced up to find him staring at her with an unreadable expression.

"You don't have to stay here." His voice sounded sincere for a change, without a hint of mockery.

She couldn't remember one time when he'd expressed any real concern for her feelings, so she didn't trust this new, unfamiliar side of him. "What do you mean, I don't have to stay?"

"You have to build a new life wherever you go. That's hard to do if you hate the place. I can take you to a safe house; tell my boss you've changed your mind. It will take some time to research alternate locations, but—"

"No, wait." She started to reach for his hand but stopped herself just short of touching him. She didn't want to see that look of disgust cross his face again.

"I'll stay. You said I'd be safe, that no one would think to look for me here. That's infinitely more important than having a Starbucks on every corner." She chewed her bottom lip. "They do have a Starbucks in Providence, right? I could really use a *Venti Mocha* right now."

He slowly shook his head, his mouth twitching. "Not that I know of."

"Oh, well. That's not important." And it wasn't, not really. The thought of going back to a safe house again, code words for cheap motel, made her cringe. After flying from New York to Nashville and riding for hours in the middle seat of an SUV, squashed between two broad-shouldered marshals, all she wanted to do was rest. They could have flown in closer to Providence, but Ryan had taken the longer route, insisting it was necessary for security reasons.

He raised a brow, waiting for her answer.

"I'll be fine. Really." Would she be fine? She didn't know, but she was willing to re-evaluate later.

He looked like he wanted to argue with her. But instead, he snapped his briefcase shut. "I'll show you how to use the alarm."

Back in the foyer he demonstrated the keypad, forcing her to set and disable the alarm several times until he was satisfied she remembered the code and how to use it.

"This red button is a panic button. It alerts the police station in town."

"But…you'll be next door, right?" She hated the fear that had crept into her voice. No doubt Ryan would seize on that and make fun of her.

"For a few weeks, yes." No sarcasm, no teasing.

Relieved, she followed him out onto the porch and watched with mixed feelings as he spoke to the marshals who'd been waiting outside. She didn't remember their names, had made a point not to.

There were already four names branded into her conscience. Along with Natalie's.

The marshals drove away, disappearing to the sound of tires crunching down the gravel road. When Jessica looked back toward Ryan, he was striding across the front lawn to his cabin next door. The rude man hadn't bothered to say goodbye. Without a word or even a glance her way, he disappeared inside, shutting the door with a resounding thud.

A cold breeze blew through the trees, ruffling Jessica's hair. She shivered and rubbed her hands up and down her arms. The sun was going down, and the temperatures up in the mountains were dropping rapidly. The trees that had looked so beautiful a few minutes ago, with their yellow and gold fall foliage, now took on a sinister cast. Shadows shifted in the bushes across the street. She could easily imagine a gunman hiding there.

Would she ever feel safe again? *Was* she safe? Ryan wouldn't have left her outside if she wasn't, would he?

The wind blew again, carrying the scent of pine trees and a host of other, unfamiliar scents and noises, robbing Jessica of the last of her courage. She turned and ran inside the house.

Chapter Four

A scream shattered the quiet of Jessica's bedroom.

Startled awake, she jumped out of bed, slammed into the dresser and fell onto the floor. Cursing the dark, unfamiliar room, she scrambled to her feet.

The noise sounded again—a short, throaty moan that echoed through the room, making Jessica wince.

Sugar. What *was* that?

Frantically feeling along the wall for the light switch, she bumped something on top of the dresser. She grabbed it to use as a weapon, and her other hand brushed against the light switch. She flipped on the light and whirled around to face whoever was in the room.

The room was empty.

She glanced around in confusion and shoved her bangs out of her eyes. The noise echoed through the room again. She nearly collapsed in relief. The noise was coming from her window, *outside* the house.

She chewed her bottom lip and debated calling

Ryan to investigate. But what if there was some logical explanation for the noise? Did she really want to endure more of Ryan's teasing if he came over and found a feral cat or some other animal howling outside?

He'd get a real kick out of that, and Jessica's pride had already taken about all she could of his *city girl* insults. More important, she was on her own now, or supposed to be. Ryan was leaving in a few weeks. She needed to learn not to panic or assume DeGaullo had found her every time something unexpected happened.

Her mind was made up, but her feet were still deciding. Blood rushed to her ears. She gathered her courage, and inched toward the window. With her back against the wall, she raised her weapon and slowly lifted the edge of the curtain.

Two round, black eyes surrounded by feathers and a beak stared back at her through the glass. Good grief, it was just a bird, sitting on her window ledge. It blinked and gave another throaty howl. As if it was satisfied that it had done its job by waking her up, it screeched again, flapped its wings and flew away.

Jessica let the curtain fall closed. She'd been scared witless by a stupid bird. Was this the kind of life she had to look forward to? Being awakened in the middle of the night by screeching birds?

The bright red numbers on the bedside clock read six-thirty. Okay, so it wasn't the middle of the night.

But since she hadn't slept well as she tried to convince herself she was safe without a marshal in the next room, it might as well be the middle of the night. She was exhausted.

She was also keyed up, full of nervous energy, so going back to bed would be just as futile now as it had been last night. She raised her hand to brush her bangs out of her eyes and only then realized she was still clutching what she'd grabbed off the dresser to use as a weapon. She stared in disbelief at what she was holding.

A blow-dryer.

Sugar.

What was she going to do if she met up with one of DeGaullo's men? Offer to style his hair?

She pitched the dryer onto the bed and trudged through the short hallway into the bathroom. Her shoulders were knotted with tension from her unpleasant wake-up call. Right now nothing sounded better than a hot, steamy shower to relax her muscles.

While she waited for the shower to get hot, she went about her morning routine. Normally she'd carefully fold her clothes and put them in the hamper, but she didn't have the energy for that right now. She discarded her clothes in a sloppy pile on the white tile floor and stepped over the side of the tub.

Icy water pricked her skin like hundreds of sharp needles. She shouted and hopped out of the tub, right onto the pile of clothes. They shot out from underneath her feet across the slippery tile. Her hands flailed in the air, futilely grabbing for the countertop. She fell hard, smacking her head against the side of the toilet.

She lay there, naked, her head throbbing, while she tried to decide whether to cry, scream, or break something. Above her, the shower curtain billowed out over the tub. Every one of the red and blue cartoon cats grinned down at her as if they were about to burst into laughter.

A strangled gurgle wheezed between her clenched teeth. She rolled over, wincing when she put pressure on her left hip. She grabbed the countertop and painfully pulled herself to her feet. When she caught sight of her face in the mirror, she let out a low groan. A dark bruise was already forming on the side of her temple.

Could this day get any worse?

All those months during the trial, she'd longed for the comforts of her apartment, her Jacuzzi tub, the fluffy down comforter she'd bought two Christmases ago during a shopping trip with Natalie. She'd hated the cheap motel rooms the government called safe houses. She'd longed for the day when she'd be in a place she could call home again.

Now that she was, she realized how good she'd had it all along. At least the cheap motels had hot water. And she certainly didn't have wild animals perched outside her window, screaming louder than

Mrs. Bailey's grandchildren when they ran up and down the hallway outside her apartment.

She shut the shower off and stood in front of the mirror, finger-combing her hair over her bruise. The tiny red scars that ran along her hairline made her pause. There were dozens of them all over her body, reminders of the explosion. Self-loathing filled her. How pathetically shallow to worry about downy comforters and jetted tubs when four men had given their lives for her.

They'd made the ultimate sacrifice, simply because it was their job, because they'd vowed to keep her safe. She was in awe of men like that, men with courage who did what was right, not what was easy. She'd worked for DeGaullo for years, too afraid to do what was right. Even the night Natalie had died, Jessica had been too scared to do anything more than cower beneath her desk. She'd done nothing to save her friend.

Her fingers tightened around the edge of the countertop. If Natalie's family, or the families of those dead marshals, could give up their modern conveniences to have their loved ones back, Jessica was certain they'd make that trade without hesitation.

So would she.

Resolved to appreciate what she had and not to complain, even to herself, she ran a sink full of cold water. She shivered through an old-fashioned washcloth bath. As she was about to leave the bathroom, the shower curtain caught her eye again.

The cats stared back at her, mocking her. Unable to resist a childish impulse, Jessica grabbed the curtain and gave it a tremendous yank. The shower rod popped off the tile and landed on the floor with a satisfying metallic clang. Jessica stomped on the curtain, ridiculously pleased to hear the plastic crinkle beneath her feet.

Feeling buoyed by her tiny victory, she dressed in a pair of jeans and a plain, blue T-shirt. The sun was up now, turning the brown curtains in her bedroom a light muddy color. Not yet ready to face the roosters marching across her kitchen walls, she decided instead to check out the view behind her house. She hurried through the living room to the breakfast nook.

No telling what was hiding behind the curtains covering the sliding glass door. Knowing Ryan, there was something awful in her backyard.

Like the city dump.

She straightened her shoulders, reached up, and slid the curtains back. Her mouth fell open at the dazzling view. The Smoky Mountains spread out before her for miles, dressed in the golds and reds of early autumn. Jessica couldn't begin to imagine how spectacular the colors might become in a few weeks when fall was in full swing. For the first time since Ryan had announced he was relocating her here, she was excited. Yes, she was a city girl, but she could still appreciate the incredible beauty in front of her.

Yesterday, hemmed in between two marshals, she hadn't had much of a chance to notice her surroundings. Today, she would take everything in and face her new life with enthusiasm. It was almost like she was eighteen again. Alone, without any family, she'd still been hopeful as she left her latest foster home to find her place in the world. This time, she wasn't that naive young woman desperate to fit in and be accepted. Her blinders were off. She would never again give her trust so easily, only to find the people she'd thought were her friends were really her enemies.

JESSICA STOOD AT the ridge-line where her backyard ended and the mountain dropped away. It wasn't nearly as steep as it had looked from her back deck. A well-worn path angled down the mountainside until it reached Ryan's house, then it angled down and disappeared into the trees below.

Those trees were so thick they blocked out the sunlight, forming a dark haven for anyone who might want to hide. Jessica rubbed her chilled arms and chided herself for worrying. She hadn't broken any of the program's precious rules. No one knew where she was. She was perfectly safe.

The sound of shoes crunching on the gravel road out front had her turning around. A large man with short, dark hair was jogging past her house. He reminded her of Ryan, but where Ryan was all muscle and brawn, this man was carrying a few extra pounds, as if he was a little too fond of his Friday-night beers.

"Morning," he called out, his voice friendly as he waved.

"Morning," Jessica automatically called back, but she was already heading toward her house to go inside. She needed to learn to face the world again, without her bodyguards, but today wasn't that day. She wasn't ready.

When the stranger saw her heading back to her house, he must have thought she was heading toward the street to meet him. He swerved into her side yard and jogged toward her.

Indecision froze Jessica in place. The safety of her house was too far away, and the stranger was almost right on top of her. She rushed backward several steps. The stranger ran forward, making a grab for her.

"No." She twisted away and kept backing up.

The man lunged for her and grabbed her arm. "Whoa, there, miss," he said. "If you back up any more you're going to fall right off the mountain." His brow wrinkled with concern.

"What?" Jessica glanced back. Her stomach dropped as she realized just how close she was to the edge. She scrambled forward and to the side, forcing the stranger to drop his hold on her arm.

"Thank you." She gritted her teeth with embarrassment. This man probably thought she was an idiot.

He raised his hands as if to reassure her and stepped back, putting several feet of space between them. "I shouldn't have run over here like that. Didn't mean to frighten you."

"No, no, you didn't do anything wrong. I'm still half-asleep. Haven't had my morning coffee yet," she joked. She glanced back toward the drop-off and shivered, wrapping her arms around her waist. A fall like that could have broken some bones, or worse. That would have been pathetic—living through a year-long trial, surviving a bombing, then falling to her death in her backyard.

A sound from next door had them both turning to see Ryan stepping outside onto his deck. He didn't seem to notice them as he leaned against the railing with a coffee cup in his hand. He stared out over the mountains, enjoying the same view Jessica had been enjoying a few minutes earlier.

"Morning, Ryan." Jessica gave an enthusiastic wave to get his attention.

He straightened, as if surprised, and returned her wave. He set his cup down on the railing and hurried across the yard toward her. His face bore an expression of polite interest when he stood next to her and looked at the stranger. "Aren't you going to introduce us, Jessica?"

"Oh, of course. Um, actually, we haven't met yet."

The man smiled at Ryan and held out his hand. "Hope I'm not intruding. I was jogging out front and saw this beautiful young lady. Just had to say hello. Mike Higgins. I'm renting a cabin down the road, about halfway up the mountain. Don't have nearly the view you two have up this high."

"Good to meet you, Mike. Ryan Jackson."

The men shook hands and Ryan gave Jessica a pointed look, clearly expecting her to introduce herself.

"Oh, I'm Jessica…ah…Benedict." She shook Mike's hand, hoping he hadn't noticed her hesitation. She'd almost said Delaney. She chewed her bottom lip and glanced up at Ryan.

He stepped closer as if to lend her his support. "You said you're staying down the road?"

"I come up here every fall, been here almost two weeks." He glanced back and forth between Jessica and Ryan. "Are you two permanent residents, or tourists like me?"

Jessica's mind went blank, all her memorized lies flying away as easily as that bird had flown away this morning. Ryan smoothed over her silence and picked up the conversation. With a straight face, he told Mike he was a seasonal tour guide for hikers following the Appalachian trail through the Smokies. He rattled off names of landmarks like Cade's Cove and something called Clingman's Dome.

Then he turned the conversation back on Mike. Apparently Mike owned a small insurance company in Little Rock, and he was anxious to get some fishing action here in the mountains. Ryan made suggestions on where Mike could catch the biggest fish this time of year.

Jessica didn't know if anything Ryan said about the area was true, but he sounded like he knew what he was talking about. If she hadn't known who he was, she would absolutely believe he'd grown up around here and that he was a professional trail guide.

As he spoke he lifted his arm and put it around her shoulders, pulling her into his side. Only then did she realize how badly she was shaking. With Ryan's warm strength supporting her, she began to relax.

It felt good being held by him—too good. It made her wish they could have met under different circumstances, before her life had gone so horribly wrong. Would he have liked her if they had? Would he have gifted her with that sexy smile that gave him a boyish, youthful look? Unfortunately, she'd never know.

"Thanks for the tips." Mike shook Ryan's hand again. "I'm going fishing real soon. Hopefully I'll catch something big." He gave Jessica a broad wink.

Ryan's arm tensed around her shoulders. Or had she imagined that? He smiled at Mike and gave him a wave. Jessica followed Ryan's lead, waving and smiling as the other man jogged back to the street.

As soon as Mike disappeared, Ryan grabbed Jessica's hand and tugged her toward her house.

"Ryan, stop. Where are you going?"

He paused at her back door. "My coffee has to be cold by now. You owe me a fresh, hot cup. Don't I smell coffee inside?" He shoved the sliding glass door back and hauled her inside, closing and locking the door behind them.

"You're acting kind of strange. What's wrong?" Her earlier unease was reawakening as she followed him into the kitchen. "Did you recognize that man?"

Ryan frowned at the empty coffeepot on the coffeemaker beside the stove. He opened the pantry and rummaged inside.

"Ryan?" Jessica repeated. "Did you recognize that man? Should I be worried?"

He turned around with a box of filters and a can of coffee and deposited them on the countertop. "Never seen him before." He pulled out the drawer next to the stove. "Is there a measuring thing in here somewhere?"

Jessica shoved his hand aside and closed the drawer. "Let me do it." She'd unpacked only a handful of boxes last night, out of necessity. The silverware was in the drawer below the one Ryan had opened.

After setting a tablespoon on the counter, she grabbed some non-dairy creamer out of the pantry, grateful that whoever had stocked her first supply of groceries had thought to include coffee. Before the trial, she'd had a habit of stopping at Starbucks every morning before work. She probably could have paid for a vacation in the Bahamas with all the money she'd spent on coffee.

"How do you take it?" she asked.

"Strong and black." Ryan moved out of the kitchen and leaned against the countertop bar, resting his forearms on the worn butcher-block laminate.

Jessica spooned coffee grounds into the filter. "I appreciate you jumping in on the conversation with Mike. I went totally blank, couldn't remember anything. I almost introduced myself using my real name."

Ryan didn't seem as appalled by that admission as she was.

"You did fine. It'll be easier next time."

Her stomach jumped at the thought of *next time*. "I hope you're right."

After starting the coffeemaker, she leaned back, taking her first good look at him since the fiasco with the stranger. Judging by the stubble darkening Ryan's face, he hadn't had a chance to shave yet this morning. His short, dark hair was slightly damp. He'd probably just finished taking a shower before he came over.

A *hot* shower, unlike hers.

"I don't suppose you know how to fix a water heater?" she asked.

He raised a brow. "Yours isn't working?"

"Nope. Unfortunately, I found that out the hard way." She gave him a rueful grin and pulled her hair back to show him the bruise on the side of her head.

His brows drew down in concern. He rushed around the countertop, stopping in front of her. His fingers gently brushed back her hair as he examined her bruise. "What happened?"

Shivering beneath his touch, she stepped back before she did something stupid, like wrap her arms around his waist and pull him closer. She shook her head at her absurd thoughts. This was *Ryan*. Maybe she'd bumped her head harder than she thought.

She rubbed her hands up and down her arms, hoping he would think she'd shivered because she was chilled. "When the cold water hit me, I jumped out of the tub and slipped. Bumped my head on the side of the toilet."

The corner of Ryan's mouth twitched and he coughed behind his hand. "Ah, well, we can't have that. I'll see if I can solve your hot water problem."

He headed into the family room toward the foyer. Jessica realized the shower curtain was clearly visible lying on the bathroom floor. If Ryan happened to glance that way, he'd know his little practical joke had paid off. He'd know how much that ridiculous shower curtain annoyed her.

Eager to turn his attention, she blurted out, "Have you had breakfast yet?"

He looked over at her, just as she'd hoped. "Are you offering to cook?" His deep voice held a note of surprise as he paused in front of the door that led into the garage.

She was surprised, too. Cooking for Ryan wasn't something she'd ever expected to do. She barely cooked for herself, let alone someone else. What was the point of cooking when she could pop a frozen pizza in the oven? Still, the idea of doing something as normal as cooking someone else a meal sounded appealing. It had been far too long since she'd done anything that remotely resembled normal.

"I was going to fix myself breakfast, anyway," she said. Ryan didn't need to know that her version of fixing breakfast was to toast a piece of bread. "If you fix my water heater, I suppose I could make enough for two."

"Biscuits, bacon, eggs?" His expression turned hopeful.

She groaned. What had she gotten herself into? "All right, but I'm not a good cook. I only know how to make eggs one way, well done."

"I don't mind." He gave her a smug look as if it had been his plan all along to get her to cook him breakfast. Then he went into the garage.

Jessica ran to the bathroom and quickly re-hung the curtain rod. Then she hurried back to the kitchen, hoping she could figure out how to fry an egg without burning it.

RYAN SHUT THE door and dug his cell phone out of his pocket. Jessica's offer to cook breakfast had certainly surprised him. He didn't know why she'd made that offer, but he was grateful to have her busy doing something else so he could do what he needed to do—find out who Mike Higgins really was. Something about that man was making all the hairs stand up on the back of Ryan's neck.

Ryan pressed his boss's number on his phone and weaved around the car and the stacks of boxes to the far corner of the garage. As he'd suspected, the thermostat on the water heater was turned on the lowest setting. The team that had set up the house for Jessica's use had forgotten to turn the thermostat up. He turned the dial. The water heater clicked and hissed as it started heating the water.

"Alex Trask," his boss's voice sounded over the phone.

"It's Ryan." He leaned back against Jessica's car and crossed his legs at the ankles. "We might have a problem."

"What kind of problem?"

"A supposed tourist jogged up the street and introduced himself to Jessica. He said his name is Mike Higgins. He's from Little Rock on vacation. Runs a mom and pop auto insurance business called *Solid Rock Insurance*. I want to know if he's legit."

"On it." Keys tapped on a computer keyboard as Alex began his search.

Ryan drummed his fingers on the hood of the car. Hopefully, Higgins would check out. When Ryan had heard voices out his back door earlier, he'd gone out on his deck, pretending not to notice Jessica and the man in the jogging suit. He'd hoped Jessica could push through her nervousness and have her first real conversation with someone other than law enforcement since she'd joined WitSec. But when she'd waved him over, he'd realized she was too nervous to face the stranger without him.

"All right, here's what I have so far," Alex said. "The insurance company appears to be real. They're listed in the phone book and have a standard-looking website with customer comments going back several years on the feedback page. The website also mentions that even though the owner is on vacation, the office is still open and serving customers. Does that sound right?"

"Yeah, that fits what he said."

"You aren't convinced?"

"Not sure. Anyone can fake a website. Something about him seemed…off. He didn't strike me as an insurance salesman. He's a big guy, my size, and he didn't look the type to sit behind a desk eating donuts all day."

"Hey, my uncle sells insurance. He doesn't sit around eating junk food all day, either."

"My point is that he makes me nervous. As he was leaving, he made a comment about going fishing, hoping to catch something big. There was something in his eyes, his voice. Sounded more like a threat."

"Where is he now?"

Ryan crossed to the end of the garage and peered out one of the rectangular glass panes in the top of the garage door. "If we can believe his story, he jogged back down the mountain to his cabin."

"I'll dig some more, call the phone numbers on the website, see if I can get a picture of the owner to email to you. But as of now, I don't see any red flags, no reason to pull the witness out."

Irritation flashed through Ryan, but he tamped it down. His boss had field experience working with witnesses. Ryan didn't. Before following the family tradition of going into law enforcement, he'd spent over a decade in covert operations as an army ranger. Everyone he'd met was either trying to kill him or was willing to sell information to someone else who wanted to kill him. Trust didn't come easily to Ryan, especially after the way his last mission had ended. His boss might be right, but Ryan wasn't taking any chances.

"Send me that picture as soon as you get it. But if that guy comes back before you can confirm his identity, I'm pulling the witness."

RYAN LEANED FORWARD under the showerhead, both hands braced against the tiles, as hot water sluiced over his head and down his back. After Jessica had cooked, or more accurately, *burned* breakfast, Ryan had spent the rest of the day hauling boxes from her garage to various parts of her house and helping her unpack. She'd seemed wary of his offer to help at first, as if she couldn't believe he was actually being nice to her.

A twinge of guilt shot through him. Jessica had every right to be wary. He'd never been especially friendly to her. And she was right to suspect he had an ulterior motive. He'd helped her unpack so he could stay with her in case Higgins returned. But he didn't want her to know that. He'd explained his actions by saying that he wanted to hurry and get her settled so he could return to New York.

She'd had no trouble believing that.

Higgins hadn't returned. And Alex had verified the insurance company's phone numbers. He'd spoken to the receptionist who verified the owner was vacationing in Providence. So far Ryan hadn't received the picture his boss had promised to email him, but the general description the receptionist had given matched the jogger from this morning.

Maybe Ryan's internal radar was screwed up. He'd been out of the military for over six months, and he usually worked behind the scenes for the marshals, planning security details. Not having to dodge bullets or be on guard every day must have dulled his instincts. All the facts pointed to Mike Higgins being exactly who he'd said he was, a businessman getting away for a few weeks of fishing and relaxation.

Ryan shook his head. Higgins wasn't the problem at the moment.

Jessica was.

Ryan had spent hours watching her curvy little bottom bending over boxes. He'd watched her pink tongue dart out to moisten her equally pink lips. He'd accidentally brushed against her when he helped her make sandwiches for lunch. And later, when she'd reached up high to put something on a shelf, he'd watched in agony as her T-shirt tightened over her generous breasts. He was in his own private little torture chamber, lusting after a woman he had no intention of sleeping with.

Ever.

Even though he desperately wanted to.

His irrational attraction for her was something he'd just have to deal with. Unfortunately, it looked like he'd be dealing with that a lot longer than he'd originally planned. When he'd asked Alex this afternoon how much longer he'd have to stay in Tennessee, his boss had dropped a bombshell.

Instead of watching over Jessica for a few weeks, which by itself was unusual in WitSec, Ryan was assigned to watch over her indefinitely.

That didn't make sense. Jessica was settled in her new location. She didn't need a marshal hanging around. That certainly wasn't standard procedure. So why did Alex insist that he stay? Something wasn't right. From the moment Ryan's boss had yanked him off another case and ordered him to deliver papers to the courthouse the day of the explosion, nothing had felt right.

Ryan closed his eyes and rinsed his face under

the spray of water. He froze when the cold muzzle of a gun pressed against the side of his head.

His eyes flew open and the shower curtain jerked back to reveal two men. Ryan didn't recognize the first man, but he definitely recognized the grinning face of the man holding the gun.

Mike Higgins.

"Hey, *Marshal.*" Mike's grin broadened. "Remember me?"

Chapter Five

Jessica put her toothbrush away, flipped off the bathroom light, and padded in her favorite New York Yankees nightshirt to her bedroom. Hopefully, she wouldn't have any visits from noisy birds outside her window tonight. She was worn out from unpacking boxes all day. She hadn't planned on unpacking the entire garage all at once, but Ryan had insisted. Since he'd done all the heavy lifting, she couldn't exactly complain.

She was still puzzled by his behavior. Prior to today, she couldn't remember one time when he'd spent more than fifteen minutes with her at any one stretch, not unless he had to, anyway. Other than stepping outside to take some phone calls several times today, he'd stayed near her every minute. He didn't seem to want to leave. If she hadn't started yawning, he'd probably still be here.

She was just sliding into bed when a bright orange light flashed outside the window, followed by a dull roar. Even without lifting the heavy curtains, she could see the flames flickering on the other side of the glass.

A bubble of panic swept through her. Jumping out of bed, she ran through the house to the front door. When she grabbed the doorknob, she yelped and yanked her hand back from the searing heat. With more caution, she held her palm a few inches from the door. Heat radiated toward her in waves. The front porch must be on fire too!

A sick feeling flashed through her stomach. Unable to suppress a whimper of fear, she ran to the set of sliding glass doors by the breakfast nook just as a wall of flames shot up from the deck.

Trapped!

No. She was not going to burn to death. There had to be a way out. She ran to the garage entry door, but it was already warping from the heat, bulging in toward the foyer.

Someone was trying to burn her alive.

Frantic, she sprinted toward the spare bedroom. *Please, please, let the windows be clear.*

As she raced into the room, the window exploded, raining glass down on the floor and shooting flames onto thc comforter. Searing heat blasted at her as the fire greedily consumed the bedding and spilled over onto the carpet. Her eyes stinging from the smoke, she ran into the hallway, slamming the bedroom door behind her.

The air in the house was already thick and hot, turning black. Coughing, gasping for air, she crouched down beneath the heavy curtain of smoke. Tears streamed down her face from her stinging eyes as she crawled on her hands and knees to the middle of the family room.

Had she really survived everything she'd been through to die like this? There had to be a way out. If she filled the bathtub with water could she survive the flames? She didn't see how she could, but it was the only thing she could think to try. When the flames got too hot, she'd sink beneath the water. Better to drown than to burn.

She started to crawl back toward the bathroom when the sliding glass doors exploded. She ducked, expecting to feel shards of glass raining down on her.

"Jessica, where are you?" Ryan's voice yelled.

Ryan? He was here? How had he gotten inside past the flames? "Ryan." She tried to yell, but she choked on the lungful of smoke she'd just inhaled. She coughed and tried to clear her throat.

Ryan appeared in front of her. She could barely see him as he pulled her to her feet and wrapped a soggy blanket around her.

"We have to run through the flames." His deep voice was as calm as if they were about to go on a sightseeing trip. He grabbed her around the waist and guided her toward the breakfast nook.

She balked when she realized he was pulling her toward the sliding glass doors, or where the doors used to be. Now there was a gaping hole of shattered glass. A curtain of flames danced across the deck in front of the opening. The only thing keeping the flames from racing into the room was the tile floor.

He grabbed a placemat from her table and used it to rake the broken glass away from the doorway. "Come on. This is the only way out."

"No, I can't." She shook her head and tried to tug away from him. The flames were so hot she felt like she was already burning.

He reached down and flipped the end of her blanket over her head, completely covering her. Her breath left her in a whoosh when he threw her over his shoulder, crushing her against him. He seemed to back away from the heat, toward the family room. Then he was running, and the heat seared Jessica even through the blanket. She screamed but the wet blanket muffled her cries. Ryan twisted violently beneath her.

They hit something solid with a bone-crunching thud. Then they were rolling, over and over until they finally came to a stop. Everything hurt, but she wasn't on fire. Ryan flipped the blanket back from her head. She gasped as she realized they were both lying on the grass twenty feet from the inferno that used to be her back deck.

Ryan must have jumped with her through the flames where the sliding glass doors had been. He'd hurtled both of them over the railing.

A section of the roof caved in, sending up a shower of sparks as part of the back of the house imploded.

"Hurry, we've only got a few minutes," Ryan said.

A few minutes until what?

He peeled the wet blanket off her. As Ryan stood, Jessica realized he was wearing a blanket, too. He shucked it off and Jessica drew in a sharp breath at the sight of his golden skin reflected in the firelight. His lack of clothing didn't seem to bother him. Then she noticed his hair, short and spiked. Singed.

"You're burned," she exclaimed. She reached up to check his scalp but he ducked away, grabbing her hand and hauling her to her feet.

"Come on." His voice was an urgent whisper. He tugged her behind him and took off in a jog toward the line of trees at the back edge of her property.

The darkness swallowed them up, and Ryan hugged the tree line with her in tow, running toward his house. He didn't stop until they were standing in his bedroom. Jessica coughed, trying to clear her lungs from the smoke she'd inhaled. Ryan, seemingly unaffected, dropped to his knees in front of a closet and began shoving things into a large backpack that was already stuffed half-full, as if he made a habit of being packed for an emergency.

There were no lights on in the house, but Jessica could easily see everything in his bedroom because of the light from the flames next door reflected in the windows.

She looked back at him. "Shouldn't you put some clothes on?" she blurted out.

He tossed the backpack onto the floor beside the

bed and rushed across the room to what she assumed must be his master bath.

For a moment, the horror of what she'd just gone through faded as she gaped at the raw, male beauty displayed so boldly in front of her. Toned muscles rippled beneath Ryan's tanned skin. Like Adonis, he was sheer perfection.

In every way.

She swallowed hard and forced herself to look at his face. "What are you doing? Shouldn't we call the fire department or something?" She stepped to the doorway, shivering in her wet nightshirt. She gasped. Two men were lying on the floor, their faces turned away from her. Rivulets of blood seeped across the tile. Jessica jerked back onto the carpet and stood next to Ryan's bed, her chest heaving, desperately trying to make sense of what she'd just seen.

Ryan grabbed some more items from a drawer in the bathroom and shoved them into a small leather case. He moved past her, threw the case in the backpack and zipped it closed. He yanked a pair of jeans off a hanger in his closet and pulled them on. Then he grabbed a thick wad of cash out of his top drawer and shoved it into his front jeans pocket. Three small rectangular boxes went into his backpack. Seeming to reconsider, he grabbed a fourth box and put that in as well.

Jessica swallowed hard. The word "ammunition" had been written on those boxes.

"Are…are those men…dead?" Jessica whispered. She clutched her throat, fighting a wave of nausea.

"It was them or me." Ryan shoved his feet into a pair of boots. He thrust his arms into a long-sleeved black shirt and yanked it down over his head. As he pulled on his coat, he frowned at Jessica.

He yanked another drawer open and pulled out some clothes. After tossing them on the bed, he reached down and grabbed the hem of Jessica's wet nightshirt. By the time she realized his intentions, he'd already whisked her shirt off. She frantically tried to shield herself, but Ryan impatiently pushed her arms out of the way and yanked a dry, long-sleeved sweatshirt over her head. Jessica froze, shocked at what had just happened, but Ryan was already reaching for a pair of sweatpants on the bed beside her.

"I'll do it." She grabbed the pants from him.

"The wet underwear has to come off, too."

"Then turn around."

Ryan's mouth quirked up in a half grin. He turned around and dug back into the closet.

Jessica quickly shucked off her wet panties and shoved them under one of the pillows on the bed. Her face flaming, she tugged on the pants, rolling the waist down several times to get a better fit. They were far too big and she had to hold them up to keep them from falling off, but they were dry, and warm.

Ryan turned around, pitching a pair of socks on

the bed. He frowned at the sweatpants and bent down, rolling up the pant legs to reveal her feet.

"Put these on." He dropped a pair of tennis shoes on the floor in front of her and grabbed another coat from the closet.

Jessica stared dumbly at the socks and shoes. The indignity of Ryan stripping her clothes faded as the image of the two dead bodies on the bathroom floor crept back into her mind. There was so much blood. She twisted her fingers in the soft sweatshirt that hung to her knees and glanced back toward the bathroom.

Swearing, Ryan grabbed her around the waist and roughly set her on the bed as if she were a child. He tugged the socks onto her feet then shoved her feet into the tennis shoes and tightened the laces.

Jessica watched him put a jacket on her and roll the sleeves up to expose her hands, as if she was seeing him through a long tunnel, as if this was happening to someone else. The far-off whine of a siren had her looking back toward the window.

Ryan lifted her off the bed and set her on her feet. "Let's go."

He tugged her arm and she stumbled after him, holding up her pants, trying not to trip as the over-size shoes flopped on her feet. Ryan didn't release her hand until they were in the garage next to a motorcycle. He shoved his backpack into the leather holder on the left side and put a smaller bag in the holder on the other side of the bike. Saddlebags, that's what they were called, right? Jessica couldn't concentrate, couldn't focus. Why were they even in Ryan's garage? The sirens were much louder now. Shouldn't she and Ryan be outside waiting for the firemen?

Ryan hopped on the motorcycle and leaned over and shoved a helmet onto her head. He tightened the strap beneath her chin. Jessica slapped at his hands when he reached for her.

"What are you doing? We have to wait for the firemen, and the police." The thought of going outside again, being so exposed, had her throat tightening. She couldn't do it.

"Jessica, we can't stay here. We have to leave. Now."

"No. I'm not going anywhere."

"If you stay here, you're dead."

She swallowed hard. "The police—"

"Won't protect you from assassins."

"Assassins? But, those men in your bathroom, weren't they the ones who started the fire?" Her heart pounded and her fingers twisted the fabric of her jacket.

His dark eyes stared intently into hers. "No, they weren't. There were two more gunmen in front of your house when I went to get you. That's why we hugged the tree line at the back of your yard when I brought you over here, so they wouldn't see us. Do you know why they were waiting in front of your house?"

"I…I don't know."

"Yes, you do. They were waiting to make sure you didn't come out of your house alive. When they go around back and see our tracks, they'll come here looking for you. We need to get out of here. Now."

She shook her head again. "No, it's not possible. I didn't tell anyone. Don't you see? I didn't break the rules. They couldn't have found me. You have to be mistaken." Her voice broke on the last word. She knew she was being irrational, but she couldn't seem to stop blubbering.

The urgency left Ryan's face and his expression smoothed out. His mouth curved into a reassuring smile. He calmly held out his hand, palm up, and waited as if he had all the time in the world. "You're right. It's not your fault. You did exactly what you were supposed to do. You didn't break the rules. I'm still here. And I'm going to keep protecting you." His voice was soothing, cajoling.

Hot tears ran down Jessica's face. "I don't know what to do," she whispered.

"I do. Take my hand. Trust me."

Jessica looked into his eyes, so intent, so certain. The paralyzing fear began to loosen its hold. This was Ryan. He'd realized the danger at the courthouse before anyone else. He'd saved her from her burning house. A peaceful calm swept through her. She stopped shaking.

"I trust you, Ryan." She placed her hand in his.

His brows drew down in a frown. He stared at her as if he was trying to figure something out, as if he was trying to figure *her* out.

The sirens had stopped. Lights flashed red and yellow through the garage windows, spurring Ryan into action. He lifted Jessica onto the bike behind him and pulled her arms around his waist.

"Ryan, wait. Where's your helmet?"

"On your head. Now, hold on tight."

He started the engine. It was nearly deafening in the enclosed space. The bike jerked forward. Jessica gasped and clutched Ryan to keep from falling off. He rode through the house, through the open back door, heading toward the back deck stairs. Jessica's eyes widened and she grasped him even tighter. The bike bumped down the steps and shot across the yard.

Jessica risked a glance back and saw a fire engine and a tanker truck on the road in front of her house. The firemen didn't even glance their way. The roar of the fire must have masked the sound of the motorcycle.

A flash of movement had Jessica looking back to her left. Two men burst forward out of the trees beside Ryan's house. One of them raised his hand and the moonlight glinted off the gun he held.

Jessica clung tighter to Ryan. "Those men—"

"I know. Get down. Lock your arms around my waist." He leaned hard to the left. The bike skidded sideways as he made a sharp turn directly toward the gunmen. They both dove to the side, out of the bike's path. Jessica bunched her fingers around the front of Ryan's leather jacket as he whipped the bike back toward the right, aiming the powerful machine at a break in the trees.

The sound of gunfire erupted behind them. The bike's engine roared. Ryan and Jessica surged over the ridge.

Chapter Six

The motorcycle plunged over the side of the mountain.

Jessica clung tightly to Ryan as the ground rushed up to meet them.

The bike landed hard, bouncing and twisting like a bucking horse trying to throw off its riders. Jessica's head banged against Ryan's back and the force of the blow, even with the helmet on, snapped her chin. The taste of blood filled her mouth from where she'd bitten the inside of her cheek.

Ryan managed to keep the motorcycle upright and gunned the engine, evening out the ride and propelling them down the path deep into the cover of trees.

Shouts sounded behind them up on the ridge, but Jessica didn't risk looking back. She was too busy trying not to fall off the motorcycle.

Ryan yelled something at her, but she couldn't make out what he'd said over the sound of the engine and the blustery wind rushing past her.

"What?" she yelled.

He turned his head to the side. "Are you okay?"

"We just jumped off a cliff. I'm peachy," she shouted back.

He swerved to avoid a tree branch.

Jessica dug her nails into his jacket. "*Sugar.* Could you warn me next time?"

"Did you just call me sugar?"

"Not in this lifetime," she growled back.

He laughed and leaned the bike to the side to dodge another tree branch. The crazy man was actually having fun. Jessica hid her face against his back, desperately hoping the wild ride would be over soon.

It wasn't.

Hours passed as Ryan rode the bike deeper into the mountains. At first, the trail they followed was well-worn, obviously heavily traveled. Then he turned onto a smaller trail, if it could be called that. There wasn't much room to maneuver and several times he had to dodge to avoid a fallen tree or a group of vines.

Jessica was proud of herself that she hadn't fallen off yet, but if they continued much longer she would have to beg for a break. Her hands were aching from the cold and from clinging to Ryan's waist for so long. She didn't know how anyone could actually enjoy riding a motorcycle. They were horribly uncomfortable, not to mention loud.

The sky was beginning to lighten to a pale gray

when Ryan pulled to a stop next to a small shack and cut the engine. The sudden silence was unnerving, but was quickly replaced by a chorus of singing crickets and chirping frogs. Jessica had heard somewhere that as long as you heard animal noises in the forest, there was no one else around. She hoped that crickets and frogs qualified as animal noises, and that she and Ryan were safe here.

"What is this place?" she asked, somewhat in awe of the Norman Rockwell appeal of the weathered shack set against a backdrop of fall foliage, and the homey scent of pine trees.

"An abandoned shed. There used to be a barn and a house to go with it a few decades ago. There are hundreds of these old structures throughout the Smokies."

"How do you know there used to be a barn and a house?"

"I didn't randomly agree with Alex to locate you in this part of the country. I did my research, memorized maps of the area. I know what's around here. Stuart Lanier, one of the rangers who served in the Army with me, lives a couple hours north. We've hiked all over the Smokies."

"So, what you're saying is that you located me here because you thought someone might come after me and we'd have to escape into the mountains?"

He shook his head. "I didn't plan on being here

at all. I planned on high-tailing it back to New York as soon as I could, but my boss didn't agree."

Jessica stiffened. It kind of sucked having a gorgeous man tell you he was only with you because it was his job.

"I studied the area," Ryan continued, "so I would know what was around, what posed a threat. I used that information to help decide if it was a safe location for you. Can you slide off or do you need help?"

"What? Oh…no, I don't need help." *Hopefully.*

She pulled off the helmet, handing it to him as she gingerly tested the inside of the cheek she'd bitten during their wild ride. Her thigh muscles screamed in agony when she swung her leg over the seat. Instead of twenty-eight, she felt closer to sixty. She hobbled backward, rubbing her lower back.

Ryan hopped off the bike as if he'd only been riding for a few minutes. Jessica rubbed her bruised posterior and glared at him with resentment. Except for the slightly singed hair, he looked like he always did—fresh, ready to take on any challenge, no worse for wear in spite of everything that had happened. He even smelled good, outdoorsy, whereas she could still smell the smoke clinging to her hair.

"Stay here." His voice was hard and cold again, as he firmly moved her away from the door of the shack and went inside. So much for the kinder, gentler Ryan she'd glimpsed when he'd talked her through her fears back in his garage. Or when he'd seemed genuinely amused when she'd used *sugar* as a curse word.

When he emerged from the shack, he held the door open for her, his gaze darting around the trees as if he expected someone to jump out at them at any moment.

Jessica followed his gaze, beginning to feel uneasy again. "You don't think they could have followed us, do you? They were on foot. They couldn't have caught up to us." She glanced up at him for reassurance. "Right?"

His jaw tightened. "Right."

He didn't sound convinced. He raised a brow, waiting for her to enter the shack. She sighed and stepped inside.

The cabin, if it could be called that, boasted one grimy window on the rear wall that barely allowed any light in. Wooden crates were scattered around the floor as if someone had used them for chairs. But there was nothing else, not even a bathroom, a convenience Jessica was sorely in need of at the moment.

Ryan stepped inside and closed the door behind him. He swept past Jessica, startling her by grabbing her hand and tugging her toward one of the overturned crates.

"What are you—"

He pressed her shoulders, forcing her down onto the crate before squatting down in front of her, his gaze at eye level with hers.

She wrinkled her brow in confusion. Was he worried about her? Did she have some blood on her mouth from biting her cheek? She wiped her mouth. No blood. "Ryan, what's wro—"

"What, exactly, did you do to Richard DeGaullo?"

Jessica's spine stiffened at the raw accusation in Ryan's voice. That intense look in his eyes wasn't concern. It was suspicion. She should have known better. Just because he'd saved her life didn't mean he'd begun to respect her. To him she was just *city girl,* the woman he'd been forced to watch over.

"You're seriously asking what *I* did to *him*? He killed my friend, right in front of me. And, oh gee, I had the gall to testify against him." She curled her fingers around the edge of the crate. "Why are you asking me this?"

"Did you steal from him?"

"What? No, of course not."

"Date his best friend, one of the other mafia bosses?"

"Are you crazy?" She shoved at his chest, but he didn't budge. "I didn't even know any of his friends, let alone some other mafia boss. I'm…I *was*…an accountant, sometimes a computer hacker. A geek. I worked in an office with four other women. De-Gaullo didn't even know my name. I probably saw him half a dozen times in the five years I worked for him. Why are you asking these questions?"

She shoved at him again, but he grabbed her hands and held them trapped in his.

"The only reason I'm alive right now is because a man was stupid enough to hold a gun to my head, and I was able to head-butt the gun and grab it. If he'd held the gun a few feet away, I probably wouldn't have made it out of my shower. And you would have burned alive in your cabin. Now it's up to me to keep you alive. And I can't protect you if I don't know what I'm up against. Answer me truthfully. Were you Richard DeGaullo's lover?"

She gasped and tugged her hands, stomping her foot in frustration when he wouldn't let go. He stared at her intently, waiting, as if she was going to confess some terrible sin. She felt like a teenager again, her latest set of foster parents accusing her of something one of the other kids had done. After all, Jessica was the one who came from bad stock—a mother who'd died a thief and a junkie, a father on death row for a murder he'd most certainly committed.

Ryan was no different, thinking the worst of her, like everyone else had her entire life. Never mind that she'd worked two, sometimes three jobs to put herself through community college. Never mind that, when she started her first job after graduation, she didn't even realize the company who'd hired her was owned by the DeGaullo crime family.

"Answer me, Jessica." Ryan lightly shook her fisted hands.

"No! I was never Richard DeGaullo's lover." She tugged her hands again but he still wouldn't let go.

She flushed hot, gritting her teeth. "Let go of me or I swear you're going to walk funny for a week." She raised her foot and pressed her sneaker between his legs.

He grimaced and released her hands.

Jessica dropped her foot and scrambled off the crate, desperate to escape Ryan's accusations, but even more desperate to take care of her painful bladder. She grabbed at the waistband of her sweatpants before they could fall to her knees, and shoved her bangs out of her eyes. "Don't follow me."

His knowing look made her face flush even hotter.

"Don't go out of sight of the cabin," he said. "If you're not back in five minutes, I'm coming after you."

She mumbled something beneath her breath that was definitely *not* sugar, and flung the door open. Her dramatic exit was ruined when she tripped on her floppy shoes. She caught herself against the doorjamb, glared at Ryan, and slammed the door.

RYAN GRINNED AS the sound of the slamming door echoed through the shack, but his grin faded as he remembered the shattered expression on Jessica's face when he'd asked her about being DeGaullo's lover. He hadn't expected that wounded doe look in her eyes, either. And he certainly hadn't expected to feel like such a heel for even asking her those questions.

She'd surprised him, looking so appalled, so offended, so…innocent. With her curves and sultry, pouting mouth, he'd assumed all along that DeGaullo would have made her his mistress. Who would have thought that sexy little Jessica was just as disgusted by that thought as he was? She seemed to be telling the truth, but nothing added up.

Mike Higgins, or whatever his real name was, had known Ryan was a marshal. He knew Jessica was a protected witness. He couldn't have known that unless he'd received inside information. The unmistakable conclusion was that someone had infiltrated WitSec, a feat which, as far as Ryan knew, had never been done before.

Richard DeGaullo had lost a tremendous amount of clout with the other mob bosses by being in the Justice Department's crosshairs during the money laundering and murder investigation, and subsequent trial. DeGaullo hadn't been able to make a move without an FBI agent shadowing him. So why would he risk placing himself back under their scrutiny, unless his gripe against Jessica was personal?

If Jessica was telling the truth, and there wasn't anything personal between her and DeGaullo, then maybe someone else was behind the leak at WitSec. But who would have the motive, or the power, to infiltrate a program whose very existence was built on the premise of absolute secrecy and unimpeachable security? And why?

This whole mess was a frustrating puzzle, and

Jessica would pay the ultimate price if Ryan couldn't piece that puzzle together—fast.

He reached into his jacket pocket and pulled out his cell phone, and the battery pack he'd removed last night to ensure no one could trace his location. Without knowing who the mole was inside WitSec, calling his boss didn't seem like the brightest idea. Alex Trask was no slouch. As soon as Ryan called, Alex would put a trace on the call.

But what other choice was there? Ryan needed to know if he could trust Alex. Calling him was a risk he'd have to take. He'd keep the call short, hopefully too short to trace.

He noted the exact time on his watch, down to the second, and made a mental calculation of just how long he thought he could safely remain on the phone. Countdown starting…now.

He snapped the battery pack on and punched the contact number for his boss.

"Alex Trask."

"It's Ryan Jackson."

"Ryan, what in blazes is going on? Where are you? Where's my witness?"

The fine hairs on the back of Ryan's neck stood straight at attention. How did Alex know that he and Jessica were on the run? The local police didn't know Jessica was a protected witness, so they wouldn't have notified the Feds. And Ryan wasn't due to place another check-in call with his boss for several more hours.

"What are you talking about?" Ryan hedged.

"Don't give me that. Your witness's house burned down last night, and rather than call me and get a team of marshals to extract her, you've both gone missing. We've also got two dead guys at your cabin. I don't have to wait for ballistics to know who killed them. You'd better start explaining."

Ryan glanced at his watch. "How did you know about the fire?"

"What? Now, listen here. Don't you start interrogating me. I need answers. You wouldn't believe the pressure coming down from the higher-ups. Where are—"

"How did you know about the fire?" Ryan repeated.

Alex cursed into the phone. "Someone staked a copy of *The New York Times* on the witness's lawn, the same edition that was published right after the mistrial. That got the local PD's attention, and the press, I might add. The police contacted the FBI, who then contacted me. Enough stalling. What's going on? Is the witness okay?"

The cabin door opened and Jessica stepped inside, clutching the waistband of her baggy sweatpants. Her eyes widened when she saw Ryan on the phone.

He held his finger to his lips to signal her to be quiet.

"She trusted WitSec to keep her identity and location a secret," Ryan said. "She was almost roasted alive. You tell me. How do *you* think she is?"

Jessica's face paled, making her eyes stand out in stark contrast. She moved to one of the crates a few feet away and sat very still, watching him.

A loud sigh sounded over the phone. "I understand your frustration. And I guess I can understand your suspicions, even though I don't appreciate it. But you can trust me, Ryan. I'm in D.C. at FBI headquarters right now. We've got everybody who's anybody looking into this. In the meantime, there could be men in the mountains already searching for you two. You've got to come in. Tell me where you are and I'll send someone to pick you up."

"Tell me who the mole is and I'll bring the witness in," Ryan said, glancing at his watch again. He needed to end the call. He and Alex were careful not to use Jessica's name, but if someone was listening to this call, they wouldn't have to be a genius to figure out who "the witness" was.

"*You* don't get to make demands," Alex fumed. "I want her back in protective custody in twenty-four hours or you'll face charges, starting with obstruction of justice."

Ryan hung up and snapped the battery pack off the back of the phone.

"Who was that?" Jessica asked, as Ryan shoved the pieces of the phone into his pocket.

"My boss, Alex Trask. I called to see if he knows who leaked your location."

"Does he?"

"Not that he's admitting, no."

"You don't believe him?"

He shrugged. "I haven't decided yet."

Jessica rubbed her hands up and down her arms, hugging her jacket tighter. "I don't understand any of this. How did DeGaullo figure out where I was?" Her skin stretched taut across her cheekbones. The strain of the past few hours was beginning to show.

"Someone inside WitSec leaked your information. If DeGaullo isn't the one who's after you, then whoever is behind this is framing DeGaullo. Does anyone else have a reason to want you dead?"

Her pink lips parted in surprise. "Are you saying someone *else* is trying to kill me?"

"That depends on whether you're hiding something from me."

Jessica fisted her hands beside her on the crate. "I'm not hiding anything."

Ryan wanted to trust her, but everything he knew about her told him he couldn't. "I wouldn't have thought DeGaullo had enough influence to get someone inside the Justice Department to help him. He'd have to have some pretty bad dirt on someone to make them do that. Or offer an equally incredible favor in return."

He crouched down in front of her again and put his hands on her shoulders, anchoring her in place. "Give me one reason to trust you. Tell me why

DeGaullo would risk everything for revenge against a former accountant he barely knew. Why does he really want to kill you?"

Chapter Seven

Jessica's lips flattened and she shoved his arms off her shoulders. "Maybe he just doesn't want to spend the rest of his life in prison." She fairly spit the words at him. "If you'll remember, he wasn't found not guilty. The trial ended in a hung jury. The Justice Department can retry him at any time. If they do, they'll need me to testify again."

Her face was alarmingly pale. And in spite of her fiercely uttered words, it was all bravado. She was shaking, and she looked so lost, so vulnerable, that Ryan had the sudden urge to pull her close, to wrap his arms around her and hold her until the color returned to her cheeks and the fear left her eyes.

He doubted she'd appreciate that gesture, since he'd just accused her of sleeping with a scumbag like DeGaullo. The fact that he even *wanted* to hold her didn't make sense. His lack of sleep must be clouding his judgment.

He clasped his hands together to keep from reaching for her, and reminded himself of what she'd done. She'd helped a crime lord launder money. She'd covered his tracks so he could spew drugs and violence into the streets of New York. That knowledge helped ease Ryan's insane urge to comfort her, if only a little.

"Are you sure there's a leak in WitSec?" she asked, squeezing her arms around her middle. "Maybe that jogger recognized me from the papers. Maybe he called a reporter, and—"

"That jogger was a contract killer. You couldn't see his face because it was turned away, but he was one of the men lying on the floor of my bathroom." He hated the way her eyes widened in fear, but he didn't have time to coddle her. If he'd misjudged the length of time it would take for a phone trace, Alex could have men zeroing in on his location right now. And the men who'd shot at him and Jessica could be following their trail, too.

"Higgins knew I was a marshal," Ryan continued. "And he knew who you were. You haven't been into town since you moved in. So unless you called someone—"

"I didn't."

"Then the only way anyone could know where you were was if they got that information from inside WitSec."

She took a minute to process that, her throat working as she swallowed. All her earlier bravado was gone. "What are we going to do?"

The desolation in her words had him gritting his

teeth. He glanced at his watch again and stood. "You have to make a choice."

Jessica shoved herself up from the crate and stared up at him, her doe eyes big and round. "What choice?" she whispered.

Ryan shoved his hands in his pockets. It was either that or grab her and try to wipe that frightened look off her face. He didn't see how the jury had let DeGaullo go when they'd seen Jessica on the stand. She had *him* half believing her and he was the last person to trust someone like her.

"First option," he said, forcing a coldness into his voice that he was, unfortunately, far from feeling, "you go back into protective custody and hope the marshals assigned to you aren't on DeGaullo's payroll."

She winced. "What's the second option?"

"Stay in the mountains with me. Let me protect you."

She swallowed and blinked several times. "Why would you do that?"

Because, for some inexplicable reason, he couldn't quite reconcile her notorious past with the forlorn woman in front of him. Right now, she seemed so innocent, so fragile. She needed him, and he couldn't stomach the thought of turning her over to someone else without knowing if he could trust them to keep her safe.

Not that he'd admit that to her. She wouldn't believe him, anyway, not after enduring all his *city girl* comments. He chose a half-truth instead. "It's my job."

Her quick nod of acceptance, acknowledging that he would only protect her because it was his job, had him clenching his jaw.

"How would you protect me?" she asked.

"We'd head deeper into the mountains and hide for a few days. Stuart, the guy I mentioned earlier, opened a private investigation and security firm after he got out of the army. He's been investigating something for me already. He won't mind looking into this as well. He has a lot of powerful contacts he groomed while still in the service, plenty of strings to pull, favors to call in. He might not be able to figure out who the mole is, but he can help us figure out who we can trust to help us."

What Ryan didn't tell her was that their only chance to elude any trackers on their trail was to go into some rough terrain, where even the motorcycle couldn't go. They'd have to hoof it from there. He hoped *city girl* could handle it. She looked like she was in good physical condition, but she wasn't used to hiking for hours on end. She also couldn't hike with clothes so big they were falling off her, and floppy shoes that tripped her up. He'd have to do something about that if she agreed to his plan.

"Where would we stay?" she asked. "How would we survive?"

The uncertainty in her voice was palpable, but she seemed to be seriously considering going on the run with him. Maybe she was tougher than he thought. Then again, maybe she just didn't realize exactly how hard the next few days could be if they stayed in the mountains. He decided to lay it all out, so she couldn't say later that he hadn't warned her.

"It won't be easy," he said. "The nights are bitterly cold in these elevations this time of year. I brought some energy bars and water, but not enough to sustain us for long. We'll have to live off the land."

A look of doubt crossed her face. "Live off the land? What does that mean?"

"No grocery stores, no electricity, no soft bed to sleep in…no bathroom." He waited for that to sink in. From the disgruntled look on her face, he guessed the *no bathroom* comment had made her decision for her.

The disappointment that flashed through him surprised him. Not that he wanted to tough it out in the mountains any more than she did, but he'd thought, for a few minutes, anyway, that Jessica was stronger than she looked. He'd thought she was more of a fighter than she'd shown so far.

She kicked the crate on the floor in front of her. "Why are you trying to talk me out of going with you? Do you think I should surrender to the marshals?"

"Do I think…wait, you still want to go with me? Even without a bathroom?"

Her face flushed an adorable shade of pink. "Surviving in the wilderness without any luxuries isn't at the top of my list of fun things to do. But it's still *surviving.* If it weren't for you, I would have died at the courthouse. And I doubt too many people would rescue me from a burning house the way you did. I'll take my chances with you."

Her little speech surprised him...again. She wasn't conforming to that neat little check box he'd marked off in his mind when he'd first met her.

"Ryan, will you get in trouble for helping me? Your boss—"

"Let me worry about him. Keeping you safe is more important."

"Why?"

He frowned. "Why what?"

She took a step closer, so close he could smell the smoke still clinging to her hair. But instead of making him want to step back, it made him want to hold her close and protect her.

"You risked your life for me last night," Jessica said. "You saved my life."

He shook his head, ready to argue with her that anyone would have done what he did, but she reached up and cupped his face with her hands.

"If protecting me means losing your job, why would you do it? Why would you continue to risk your life for me?"

The shock of her soft, warm hands on his face had his pulse picking up. His gut tightened, and his gaze seemed to drop against his will to her oh-so-tempting mouth, just inches away. All he had to do was lean down and he could capture her lips with his.

Maybe he should.

If he kissed her now, would that get this insane desire out of his system? He could satisfy his curiosity, slake this desperate need. Then maybe he wouldn't want her so badly. He wouldn't be in an almost constant state of arousal around her, as he had been all night while riding the motorcycle, her breasts burning a hole in his back every time the bike bounced over the trail. The only thing holding him back right now was the way her brown eyes stared up at him, so trusting, waiting for his answer.

He ruthlessly reined in his desires, tightening his hands into fists to keep from reaching for her and crushing her against him. She shouldn't look at him that way, as if maybe *she* wanted him to kiss her just as badly as *he* wanted to kiss her. He needed her to want him to keep his distance. He needed her to hate him. It would make everything much simpler that way.

"Ryan?" she prodded, placing her hand on his chest and frowning up at him. "Why are you helping me?"

He took a step back, forcing her to drop her hand. "I told you at the hospital that I'm honor bound to keep you safe," he said, reminding both of them why he was with her in the first place. "Now that I know that the marshals who died protecting you were double-crossed by someone inside WitSec, I've got even more reasons to keep my vow to protect you. I'm not going to let whoever leaked your identity win. I want justice."

Jessica's gaze dropped from his and he immediately regretted his harsh answer.

"I want justice, too, for the marshals, for my friend, Natalie," she said, her voice a bitter whisper in the stillness of the cabin. "And if DeGaullo wants to kill me, I'm not going to make it easy for him. I'm staying with you."

The first tiny stirrings of respect welled up inside Ryan at Jessica's brave echo of the same words he'd told her the first time he'd seen her.

Don't make it easy for him.

He unzipped his jacket and pulled his Glock out of the inside pocket.

She made no attempt to take the gun when he offered it to her. Instead, she narrowed her eyes at him. "Why are you trying to give me your gun?"

"I'm going to backtrack, disguise our trail, and see if anyone is following us. This place is isolated. It's unlikely anyone would stumble across it. But if the worst happens, you'll have to protect yourself." He held out the gun again. "There's no safety. All you do is aim and squeeze."

Jessica eyed the gun with obvious distaste. "Perhaps you didn't hear me. I said I was staying with you. You're not leaving me behind."

Irritation flashed through Ryan when he noted

the stubborn set of her jaw. He'd make much faster progress without her clinging to him, and him worrying about her falling off the bike. The woman had obviously never been on a motorcycle before. She didn't even know to lean into the curves.

"I'm not leaving you behind," he tried to reassure her. "I'll be back in a couple of hours, three tops."

"Why do you have to backtrack at all? Why can't we just keep going deeper into the mountains?"

Ryan lowered the gun, his frustration level rising as he glanced at his watch. If the gunmen were following them, how close were they now? What if others had been positioned in the mountains before the fire, ready to cut off any avenues of escape? They could be closing in right now.

"Heading into the mountains on a motorcycle wasn't the smartest thing to do," he said. "But we didn't have much of a choice last night. Even an average tracker will be able to follow our tire tracks. Plus, the bike is loud. We're okay using it a little while longer, if our pursuers aren't far enough into the mountains to hear it yet. But without knowing how many people are following us, and what directions they're coming from, I don't know what strategy to take to elude them. I need to do some scouting. If you're with me, you'll just slow me down."

"It doesn't make sense for you to have to ride all the way back here to get me once you do whatever you need to do," she countered, her words rushing together as she took a step forward. "I promise I won't interfere. Just take me with you. I'll have your back, keep an eye out so no one sneaks up on you while you do whatever you need to do."

The fear stamped on her taut face, and the way her gaze had darted toward the door and window, told him far more than the words she'd spoken. Jessica was afraid that if he left, he'd never come back. She was afraid he would abandon her.

Ah, hell. He was going to have to take her with him.

Chapter Eight

After backtracking several miles to lay a false trail, Ryan turned the bike deeper into the forest, bumping over fallen logs and working his way to increasingly higher elevations. Even though he and Stuart had hiked the main trails in this area, he'd never been in this particular section of the mountains before. He had to stop several times to consult his map and GPS tracker to navigate his way to his destination, one of the highest peaks in the Smoky Mountains National Park.

Riding all the way to the top would take far too long, and wasn't necessary. All he needed to do was find a high enough area not completely covered in trees, so he could get the lay of the land and a view of anyone pursuing them. Fortunately, today was one of the clearer days. The smoky haze that often covered this mountain range was thin enough that he'd be able to see for miles around.

When he reached a rocky rise that would allow him an unobstructed view, he parked the bike beneath a stand of trees and killed the engine.

Jessica started behind him. "Are we there yet?"

Ryan glanced back at her, steadying the bike so she could dismount. He frowned when she hid a yawn behind her hand.

"Did you actually fall asleep while we were riding?" he asked.

She blinked as if trying to focus, reminding him of one of the screech owls so common in this area. "I guess I did."

The thought of her falling off as the bike bumped over the rocky terrain made his stomach sink. "From now on, you're riding in front so I can hold on to you."

"O...kay," she slurred. She slid off the bike and plopped down on the ground. Before Ryan even had the kickstand down, Jessica had slumped against a tree, closed her eyes, and lapsed into soft snores.

So much for her *having his back* and making sure no one snuck up on him like she'd promised at the shack. Ryan grinned and shook his head.

He squatted down, unsnapped her chinstrap, and cradled her against his chest so he could take off her helmet. When he turned back to face her, he found himself in a lip-lock.

His shock turned into a shudder when her fingers curled into his jacket and her soft mouth moved against his. All his reasons for not trusting her, all the terrible things she'd done in her past, faded beneath the achingly soft fullness of her lips on his.

He groaned and clasped her to him, deepening the kiss, urging her to open her mouth.

Her head fell back and she snorted loud enough to startle a bird in the oak tree above them.

She'd fallen asleep while he was kissing her. She was probably asleep the entire time.

His ego took a dive, and his face heated. Served him right for his lack of discipline. He could picture his father and brothers shaking their heads with disapproval, berating him for dishonoring the family's generations of law-enforcement officers by consorting with the enemy.

Even if he could ignore his deep-seated family traditions, he could never reconcile himself to Jessica's past. She hadn't just looked the other way when working on the DeGaullo accounts. She had actively helped him, using her accounting skills to cover his money laundering. Ryan could never trust a woman like that. Without trust, there was nothing to build on, no common ground, no possibility of a future.

He shook his head again at his crazy thoughts. It's not like he had a choice, anyway. Once the mole in the Justice Department was found, Ryan still had to get Jessica off this mountain alive. If he managed that feat, she'd go right back into WitSec. The only way he could be with her then was if he went into WitSec too, which meant never seeing his family again.

That was one sacrifice he would never make.

For anyone.

He gently lowered her to the ground, straightening slowly while he struggled to get his traitorous body back under control. It was several minutes before he could walk again without the pleasure-pain of his erection pressing against his jeans. If Jessica had this kind of effect on him now, he couldn't imagine what touching her would be like if she were a fully active participant.

It would probably kill him.

He grinned again when she let out another loud snort and rolled over onto her side, snuffling against the pine needles.

Ryan prepared a bed of moss and leaves for Jessica to sleep on while he climbed the rocky rise a few feet away. He covered the makeshift bed with the blanket from one of the bike's saddlebags. Then he gently lifted her in his arms. He frowned at how light she was, how delicate and vulnerable she seemed. She couldn't afford to miss many meals. If they were stuck in these mountains for more than a few days, he'd have to hunt for something more substantial than granola bars to keep her strength up.

The dark circles under her eyes told him how exhausted she was, how desperately she needed to sleep, but he had to wake her, at least for a minute. He remembered how panicked she'd been at the shack when she was convinced he was trying to abandon her. If she woke up and found him gone, she might panic again.

He lowered her to the blanket and gave her a gentle shake.

"Wake up, sleeping beauty."

Her lashes fluttered open, her sleepy lids at half-mast.

"Are we there yet?" she asked, echoing her earlier words.

Ryan's fingers curled into his palms. This woman was far too adorable for his peace of mind. "I'm going to climb that rise—" he said, pointing off to his left "—to take a look around. I won't be far. I should be able to hear you if you call out, but take my gun just in case."

Having realized earlier that Jessica had a strong aversion to guns, Ryan didn't give her a chance to argue. He swiftly tucked his Glock in her jacket pocket, zipped it closed, and hurried away from that disturbingly tempting mouth of hers.

JESSICA FROWNED AND stared toward the trees where Ryan had just disappeared. When he'd woken her up, she'd been dreaming that he was kissing her. The dream was so real, his kiss so soft and gentle, it had made her pulse leap crazily in her chest and her belly tighten in response. Even now, the memory of that dream sent a delightful shiver down her spine.

For a moment, she'd thought the dream was real.

It wasn't of course. Her mind was just fuzzy,

drunk from lack of sleep, blending dreams with reality. Ryan would probably be horrified that she'd even considered that he might want to kiss her. He wouldn't want to taint himself by associating with a woman like her, a woman he considered—by his own words—almost as bad as DeGaullo.

She pressed her lips together. She was far from perfect and had made some terrible mistakes. She might not like that Ryan had prejudged her, like everyone else. But she couldn't really blame him. Maybe he was right and she *was* as bad as DeGaullo.

She rubbed her tired eyes and shifted her weight, only now realizing she was lying on a soft blanket. At least Ryan respected her enough as a human being to offer her that small comfort. She wiggled to get comfortable, and her arm bumped against the bulge caused by the gun Ryan had stuffed into her jacket pocket. Her lips curled with distaste. She'd seen firsthand how devastating a gun could be, and she loathed the necessity of having one.

A twig snapped behind her. Jessica bolted upright, clawing for the gun as she squinted into the shadows.

WHEN RYAN REACHED the crest of the rocky incline, he belly-crawled across the top. If someone was on the trails below and looked up, he didn't want them to see his silhouette against the bright blue sky behind him.

Tugging on the string looped around his neck, he pulled out his binoculars from where he'd tucked them inside his jacket. The mountains blazed with autumn color. Dozens of hiking paths snaked out in every direction, forming a network of gold lines amongst the trees.

From this vantage point, he could just barely make out the shed he and Jessica had been in earlier this morning, as well as a handful of other structures scattered around the mountain range. Most were abandoned, their doors sagging open, the aged gray wood warped or missing.

But not all of them were abandoned.

Some of them had cars parked out front, and cool-weather flowers spilling out of planters beside the front doors. Although he and Jessica had come a long way from his house, which was too far away to see, they still hadn't escaped the dangers of civilization.

He debated ditching the noisy bike, worried that the sound might carry in the mountains. But he needed to get Jessica to a more secluded, defensible position, with only unoccupied mountains at his back. The only way to get deep enough into the mountains to find a place like that, quickly, was on the bike. For now, he decided the benefits outweighed the risks. He'd hold on to the motorcycle a bit longer.

Half an hour passed and he still hadn't seen anyone following them on the trails. He risked a quick phone call to the one person nearby that he trusted, a man who'd been his best friend growing up in Colorado, and who'd fought by his side on too many missions to count—Stuart Lanier.

Stuart readily agreed to snoop around and use his contacts to try to find out who the major players in the WitSec fiasco might be.

"Tell me where you are," Stuart said. "I can send some of my men to pick you up. You can hide out at my place until this blows over."

"I'm disobeying a direct order by not turning Jessica over to the Justice Department right now," Ryan said. "I don't want to get you in trouble with the law by giving us safe haven. Just dig around, see what you can find out. That's the kind of help I need right now."

"Fair enough. But you've got my number."

"I owe you," Ryan said.

"Nah, you've saved my butt more times than I can count. Later, man."

Ryan hung up with a promise to call back tomorrow. He stowed the phone, then took one last look around. He was just about to put his binoculars away when he spotted movement. Off to the west, a few miles away, a couple walked hand in hand along the edge of a stream. Ryan traced his binoculars behind them to see where they'd come from. He located their campsite, little more than a half mile from where he was. The couple definitely wasn't roughing it. They had an enormous camper hooked to the back of their pickup truck. Next to that, they'd strung a clothesline high up in the trees with a full load of laundry drying in the sun.

Scanning back to the couple again, Ryan considered the woman's size. She wasn't quite as petite as Jessica, but she was close enough for his purposes.

Time to go shopping.

JESSICA SCREAMED AGAINST the hand covering her mouth.

"Hush, it's me, Ryan."

She slumped in relief, pressing her hand against her chest as Ryan released her.

"Why did you sneak up on me?" she whispered furiously, her embarrassment at her reaction making her voice much harsher than she'd intended.

Ryan's eyes widened and he plucked the gun from her hands. "You do realize that thing is loaded, right?" He examined the gun before shoving it into his jacket pocket.

Jessica flushed. "Well, of course I know it's loaded, not that I realized I was pointing it at you. I keep hearing noises in the woods. I've been waiting an eternity for you to come back, scared to death a bear or a mountain lion would come along and eat me."

Ryan's mouth tilted up at the corner. "Lions and bears? Were there tigers, too?"

"Do *not* make fun of me," she warned.

He held a hand across his heart in mock horror.

"Wouldn't dream of it. And I was only gone for two hours, not an *eternity*. Here." He picked something up off the ground and held it out to her.

"Clothes! Oh, my gosh, jeans and a shirt!" Jessica grabbed them from him, but her pleasure at having clean girl clothes instead of Ryan's baggy hand-me-downs faded as suspicion took hold. "Did you steal these?"

"I borrowed them without permission, but I left money to cover what I took." He pointed down at the ground. "I brought you some hiking boots, too. They might not be your exact size, but they should fit better than those floppy tennis shoes you're wearing. I got you another pair of jeans and another shirt, too. They're in the saddlebag."

Jessica squealed in delight and grabbed the boots. They were only a half size larger than what she normally wore. She grinned, so pathetically pleased that she stood on her tiptoes and kissed Ryan full on the mouth.

He stiffened and she immediately pulled back, her face heating with embarrassment. "I'm sorry. I shouldn't have done that. I wasn't thinking." She hugged the clothes to her chest and wished she could find a hole to crawl into.

"I'll give you a minute to change." Ryan's voice was oddly strained. He turned and disappeared into the trees.

Jessica plopped down on the forest floor, mortified. Twice now she'd made a fool of herself over

Ryan. First, brushing up against him in the bathroom. And just now, kissing him. What was she thinking? She *wasn't* thinking. That was the point. She was still exhausted in spite of her nap, and her brain wasn't working like it should.

She changed quickly, briefly worrying about the fact that she didn't have a bra to wear beneath the T-shirt, which stretched across her breasts like a second skin. Well, it shouldn't matter, not really, not when she'd have her coat on most of the time. And Ryan obviously didn't think about her *that* way. She could probably walk around naked in front of him and he wouldn't even notice.

She tugged her bulky jacket on. The fact that the coat was too big didn't bother her at all like the clothes had. That extra material made her toasty warm, an important concession when the cold wind whipped against her on the motorcycle.

A fallen tree became her chair as she tugged on the boots and tied the laces with quick jerks. When Ryan returned, he was pushing the motorcycle. She ignored the hand he held out to help her to her feet, preferring not to feel him stiffen in disgust again when she touched him. She could only take so much humiliation in one day.

"Did you see anyone following us?" she asked, trying to pretend the stupid kiss had never happened.

"We're safe, for now. We'll ride deeper into the

mountain range, away from the Appalachian trail so we don't meet up with any hikers."

Ryan handed her the helmet and hopped on the bike. Jessica started to get on behind him but he shook his head.

"I can't risk you falling asleep again and falling off the bike. You're sitting up here." He leaned to the side and lifted her up onto the seat in front of him before she could protest.

She barely had enough time to register how warm his arm felt around her waist, even through the jacket, before he gunned the engine, throwing her back against him. Her thighs molded to his, and her bottom rested in a very warm spot. She wiggled, trying to scoot forward, and she heard his sharp intake of breath.

"Be still, woman," Ryan warned her over the sound of the engine.

She froze, worried that she might have hurt him. Then she felt the unmistakable pressure of his growing erection. That must be his body's automatic reaction from her accidentally rubbing against him. It certainly wasn't because he desired her.

She didn't move, didn't say a word. If Ryan could ignore the fact that his erection was hardening against her, so could she. And the fact that her toes curled in response, well, she'd just have to ignore that, too.

RYAN GRITTED HIS teeth when the bike bumped over a tree branch and Jessica's warm bottom rubbed against him. If he was going to keep her alive, he had to focus. Because what he hadn't told her was that, right before he climbed down to go get her clothes, he *had* seen someone following them. A lone man dressed all in black with a rifle slung over his shoulder.

The gunman was several miles away, but he was coming up fast, too fast to see any animal tracks in the dirt. He wasn't hunting deer.

He was hunting Jessica.

Chapter Nine

Jessica didn't know how Ryan continued to function without any sleep. Despite her earlier nap, she was so tired she wanted to collapse and have a good cry.

They'd bounced around on the horrible motorcycle for what felt like forever, stopping for a few minutes at a time for a quick meal of energy bars, or a necessary private moment behind a tree, or—as was becoming his habit—for Ryan to climb up a tree with his binoculars and scan the trails below.

Every time he came back down out of a tree, his face was lined with tension and he'd urge her to get back on the bike and keep going. He was constantly turning the bike onto harder, rougher terrain instead of following the easier paths. When Jessica asked him why, he told her it helped conceal the bike's tracks. And when she'd asked him if she should be worried, he simply told her he would protect her, no matter what.

His cryptic answers weren't exactly comforting, but she didn't have much choice other than to trust him that everything was okay. Maybe he was always this tense when he was in his Witness Protection mode.

A blast of cold wind had Jessica shivering and Ryan pulling her closer against him. His protectiveness was so automatic that she doubted he even thought about what he was doing. But every time he tightened his arm around her waist or he spoke next to her ear to ask if she was okay, a little thrill shot through her.

She recognized it for what it was—lust, pure and simple—which was surprising since she'd never considered herself to be all that passionate. She craved the feel of his hot skin sliding against hers, his firm lips pressed against her mouth, his tongue thrusting in rhythm with his body as he made slow, sweet love to her.

She shivered again.

"Do you need a blanket?" Ryan raised his voice so she could hear him.

Jessica shook her head. "Aren't you ready to pass out by now? You haven't slept at all."

"I'm okay. A few more hours. Then we'll stop for the night."

Apparently, former army rangers-turned U.S. Marshals weren't capable of telling time. Ryan's *few more hours* ended up being far longer. As the sun sank lower in the sky, Jessica's thigh muscles began to cramp. Was Ryan purposely trying to torture her?

"I AM NOT torturing you."

Jessica blinked up at Ryan, surprised to find herself being carried in his arms. She must have fallen asleep when he'd climbed a ridge to scout the trail again. Being in his arms felt far too wonderful for her to tell him to put her down.

"What did you say?" She raised her arms around his neck as he stepped over a fallen tree branch.

"You were talking in your sleep. Apparently you think I forced you to ride all day just to make you miserable."

She talked in her sleep? Great. What else had she said? She hoped she hadn't told him how appealing he was, physically, anyway. Personality-wise, he was far too bossy.

Most of the time.

"We're here." He released her legs and steadied her on her feet.

She blinked again as she realized exactly where *here* was. She'd obviously been far too preoccupied staring up at him to notice her surroundings.

She was noticing them now.

"A cave, Ryan?"

"You were expecting the Hyatt, *city girl?*"

She aimed her best glare at him. "I was hoping for something better than Motel 6."

The corner of his mouth tilted up in a grin.

"Why do you call me *city girl* when you're from New York, just like me?" she asked, putting her hands on her hips.

"I don't live in that concrete jungle," he said. "I only go into the city when I have to, like the day of the mistrial." He glanced around the cave. "You'll be warmer in here than outside. And there aren't any bears in here."

She narrowed her eyes, letting him know she didn't appreciate his latest jab.

Ryan crossed to the far wall and shrugged off the backpack. After dropping it to the ground, he turned and headed back toward the cave entrance. Jessica's stomach jumped and she rushed after him.

"Where are you going?" She halted, cringing at the note of panic in her voice.

His brows drew down in a dark slash as he turned around. "I'll be right back. Why do you always assume I'm going to abandon you?"

The tightness in Jessica's chest eased. "No reason. I'm just tired. Go on. I'll be fine." She smiled, feeling like a fool.

He closed the distance between them and reached out, brushing her bangs back from her eyes.

"You're shaking." His voice mirrored his surprise. He wrapped his arms around her and pulled her close.

Jessica stiffened, but when he didn't release her, or call her *city girl,* she clutched the front of his jacket and sank into his warmth, resting her head against his chest. Several minutes passed, and when he didn't let her go, she realized he was still waiting for an explanation.

"It's stupid," she whispered. "I was a little girl. It was such a long time ago."

"Tell me." His voice was a deep whisper in the silence of the cave, a comforting rumble beneath her ear.

She squeezed her eyes shut against the memories. "I don't remember much, just…impressions. My dad, driving me to the grocery store, telling me to wait for him, that he'd be right back. I waited, and waited. Finally, the store manager took me to his office and called the police."

Ryan tensed against her. "Your father left you at a store? He never came back?"

She nodded, not trusting her voice.

"What about your mother? Didn't she come looking for you?"

The unwelcome pity in his voice had her shoving out of his arms. She laughed without humor. "I don't want to talk about this. It doesn't matter, really it doesn't. I barely even remember my parents. Sometimes, I just…I get a little nervous, that's all, when I'm alone. I overreact, I know that. I just…" She hugged her arms around her waist. "Go on, do whatever you were doing. I'll…" She looked around the tiny cave. "I'll unpack the supplies we'll need for the night."

She crossed the cave and got down on her knees in front of the pack.

"Jessica."

She tugged on the zipper and reached inside.

"Jessica."

The command laced in his voice had her frowning up at him. The man really was far too bossy.

"It *does* matter," he said. "I'll never abandon you. If I leave, I'll always come back. Got that?"

She smiled bitterly. "Don't make promises you can't keep. Everyone leaves eventually."

Ryan frowned. He opened his mouth to say something, but apparently thought better of it. He snapped his mouth shut and turned away, disappearing around the curved entrance of the cave.

WHEN RYAN STEPPED back inside the cave, pulling a pile of pine tree branches behind him, his expression was wary—as if he thought Jessica might lapse into some other crazy phobia.

She sighed, wishing she could take back her earlier confession. She'd certainly never intended to share something so personal with Ryan.

"What are you doing?" she asked, as he stacked some of the smaller branches in a ladder-like pattern on the ground next to the back cave wall.

"Making a bed."

He reached into the backpack and pulled out what appeared to be a sleeping bag, except that it was incredibly thin. He laid it on top of the branches before tossing the small blanket on top, the same blanket he'd used earlier this morning to fashion a pillow for Jessica.

"That so-called bed doesn't look comfortable," Jessica said.

"It's softer than the floor. And the pine needles act as a natural bug repellant so they won't crawl all over you while you sleep."

She crossed her arms at that nonsense. Did he think that, because she was a woman, she was afraid of bugs? Never mind that she *was* afraid of bugs. He didn't need to know that. "Don't you need more branches for the other bed?"

"One sleeping bag, one bed."

She eyed the bed dubiously and opened her mouth to protest, but he raised a brow in challenge.

"Don't waste your time arguing," he said. "In another hour the sun will set and the temperatures will plummet. The only way to stay warm is by sharing body heat."

"Couldn't you start a fire? Don't you have a lighter in that bottomless pack of yours?"

He gifted her with a sexy, lopsided grin. "The pack is far from bottomless. I didn't have time to grab everything we'd need for an extended camping trip. I do have a lighter, but we can't risk starting a fire at night. The light could be seen for miles around. That's another reason we had to stop for the night. I can't risk the motorcycle's headlights being seen."

She noted the tension in his face again. "Someone's following us, aren't they?"

He looked like he was about to deny it, but then

he said, "One man, that I've seen. Don't worry, he's miles away. We're safe here for the night."

"You're sure?"

"As sure as I can be." He reached into one of the side pockets in the backpack. "There's a stream nearby. We can bathe in the morning, but for now, this should make you feel better." He pulled out a hairbrush, toothpaste and toothbrushes.

Jessica gasped with delight and grabbed them from him. "What are we waiting for?"

He laughed and pulled her to her feet.

A few minutes later, after cleaning herself as best she could in the freezing stream, and scrubbing her teeth, Jessica felt human again. She'd never thought of a toothbrush as a luxury, but she'd never take one for granted again.

When they were back in the cave, Ryan blocked the entrance with the pile of pine tree branches. He took off his jacket and lay down on the bed. He closed his eyes, looking perfectly content. Jessica followed his lead, shrugging out of her jacket.

When she glanced over at Ryan, she realized his eyes were open again, and he wasn't looking at her face. His heated gaze was focused several inches lower. Jessica followed his gaze, then gasped and crossed her arms over her chest. She'd forgotten how tight and thin the T-shirt was.

Unapologetic, Ryan shrugged and raised the blanket. Jessica hesitated, then slid in beside him, lying on her back, staring at the ceiling.

Tension coiled inside her. Had she imagined the heat in Ryan's gaze? Probably. She certainly didn't have to imagine the answering heat inside her. Desperate for a distraction that didn't involve her crawling all over him and making a fool of herself, she blurted out, "Ryan?"

"Um?" His voice sounded sleepy.

"Tell me about yourself. All I know is that you protect people for a living, you're extremely comfortable with guns and you ride motorcycles."

He laughed, the deep sound curling through Jessica and making her ache to move closer to him.

So much for distracting herself by talking.

"You make me sound like a Hell's Angel," he said. "Or maybe a Jackie Chan wannabe."

She frowned. "Jackie Chan?"

Silence met her question. She turned her head to look at him, barely able to see him in the rapidly darkening cave. His face was only a few inches from hers and he was staring at her with a stunned expression.

"You don't know who Jackie Chan is?"

"Sorry," she said, trying not to watch his handsome mouth as it moved. "Afraid not."

"I thought everyone knew about Jackie Chan. He's a modern-day Bruce Lee."

"Bruce Lee?" she teased, knowing full well who Bruce Lee was.

Ryan groaned as if she'd mortally wounded him.

"That's just wrong. Please tell me you at least know who John Wayne is."

"Well, of course I know who he is. He's that guy who does those shows in Vegas."

Dead silence filled the cave, which was so dark now that she couldn't see his face anymore.

"Jessica?"

"Yes, Ryan?"

"Are you teasing me?"

"Maybe."

"I jump into a burning building for her and this is how she repays me. Denigrating my heroes. It's a sad world we live in."

The reminder of the house fire was like a bucket of ice water, sobering her and washing away her earlier amusement. She flipped on her side to face him. The darkness gave her courage. She reached out, her fingers brushing against his shoulder, and followed his sleeve down to his hand, entwining her fingers with his.

"Jessica," he said, his voice oddly strained. "What are you doing?"

"I've never really thanked you for saving me. I know I wouldn't have gotten out of my house alive if it weren't for you. I still can't believe you jumped through that fire for someone like me." She squeezed his hand and followed the line of his arm back up until she touched his cheek. She was so tired now that she didn't care if he stiffened against her or not. Leaning forward, she pressed a quick, soft kiss to his lips.

"Thank you," she whispered.

He didn't stiffen or pull away, but it was a long time before he spoke. "You're welcome." His voice sounded deeper than usual, but there was genuine warmth in his words, no condemnation or disgust this time.

The tension in Jessica's shoulders eased. "Will you tell me more about yourself?" she asked.

"Like what? My service number?"

"Tell me that later, when I have a pen."

He chuckled. "Short bio. I grew up on a horse ranch in Colorado with three brothers and a sister. I was in the army for ten years, got out a few months ago and became a marshal. Never been married, no kids."

"Why would you quit the army to become a marshal?"

"Tradition. Most everyone in my family goes into law enforcement eventually, in some capacity. I wanted to serve my country first, but then, after..."

She felt him shrug against her in the darkness.

"After my last tour, I felt I'd done my duty, so I became a marshal."

What was he about to say when he paused? Jessica sensed there was more to him quitting the army than he was admitting. "You said it's a family tradition to go into law enforcement. What about your mom and your sister?"

"My mom did a stint as a 9-1-1 operator. My sister's the oldest of my siblings and the first one in my generation to carry on the tradition. She's a detective, and she'd probably slug you for implying that a woman can't succeed in law enforcement."

"I didn't mean to…I wasn't trying to say, that is—"

He reached out and squeezed her hand. "Apology accepted."

Jessica felt the warmth of his hand all the way to her toes. She swallowed hard and cleared her throat. "If your family is busy chasing bad guys, who takes care of the ranch?"

"We all pitched in when we could, still do on occasion. But mostly, Mom handles the books and Dad hires ranch hands to take care of day-to-day operations. The ranch has been in the family a long time. It's a well-oiled machine."

"So, you're a cowboy-soldier-marshal who likes John Wayne and hates city life. There are a lot of holes in that bio."

"Ask me anything. I'm an open book."

"Okay. What's your middle name?"

He squeezed her hand again. "Anything but that."

"You said you were an open book."

"I am, except for my middle name. It's my cross to bear. I still haven't forgiven my mother."

Jessica laughed. "It can't be that bad. At least tell me what it starts with."

"It comes after d and before f."

"I'm guessing it's e."

"Smart lady."

"Be warned. You've whet my curiosity and I don't give up easily. I'm going to figure out your middle name."

"Not a chance," he said.

The bed of branches shifted slightly and Jessica sensed that Ryan had rolled onto his side facing her.

"Did you join the army instead of going to college?" Jessica asked.

Ryan's warm breath puffed out in a sigh, brushing across her neck. "What makes you think I didn't go to college? Do I sound uneducated?"

"No, of course not. I just thought, since you joined the army—"

"I happen to have an official piece of paper in a drawer somewhere saying I graduated college."

"In a drawer somewhere?"

"You think I should have it on my ego wall?" he teased.

"Do you have an ego wall?"

"As a matter of fact, I do."

"What's on it, if not your college diploma?"

He fell silent, and after a while, Jessica thought he might have fallen asleep.

"My wall has things that really matter," he finally said, his deep voice tinged with a hint of sadness. "Pictures of men I served with in special forces. Men who died." Another pause. "I lost four men on my last mission."

The regret and sadness in his voice tugged at her heart. "I'm sorry about your men."

He didn't answer, and after waiting for several minutes, she realized he wasn't going to. "I don't understand," she said. "How is a wall of pictures an ego wall?"

He sighed again, as if realizing she wasn't going to give up. "It reminds me not to have an ego. It reminds me that no matter how experienced or how accomplished I think I am, anything can happen. There are no guarantees."

"I'm sorry, Ryan. Sorry you lost your friends." An image of the explosion flashed through her mind. She squeezed her eyes shut, wishing she could block out her memories just as easily as she closed her eyes. "And I'm so sorry that I'm the reason your marshal friends died." She rolled to her other side, facing away from him.

He wrapped her in a bear hug, shocking her as he pulled her tightly against him, spooning his body behind hers. "The explosion wasn't your fault," he whispered. "I never should have blamed you for that. I'm the one who owes you an apology. I'm sorry, Jessica."

He reached out until he found her hand again and he entwined his fingers with hers. He gave her a gentle squeeze and held her close. For a long moment, Jessica lay there, shocked that he'd apologized and that he continued to hold her close, offering her the comfort of his arm around her waist.

Her heart nearly broke as a wave of longing crashed over her, swamping her with emotion. Not lust this time, although her desire for him was always there, simmering beneath the surface. No, this time she longed for acceptance. She longed for Ryan to care about her, to want to protect her because he liked the person she was instead of just because it was his job. She longed for a real family, like Ryan's—brothers and sisters, a mother and a father who would love her, and never leave her.

She longed for a way to make up for all the pain she'd caused so many people because of the choices she'd made in her life. She wanted to have value. She wanted to matter to someone.

And she wanted to hear Ryan's laugh one more time before she went to sleep.

"I know what the *e* stands for," she said, her voice hesitant. She waited for his response. One heartbeat. Two.

"What does it stand for?"

Relief swept through her. "Everett," she teased.

"Nope."

"Elrod?"

He chuckled. "No."

The vise around Jessica's heart eased at the sound of his laughter. "Ernest?"

"Not even close."

"I've got it. Elbert."

"No, my middle name is not Everett. It's not Elrod, or Ernest, and it most certainly is not Elbert."

She heard the smile in his voice and she smiled in return. "Good night, Ryan."

"Jessica," he said, his voice serious again. "I'm going to wake you at first light. I wish I could let you sleep longer, but we need to put some more distance between us and that gunman. Once we get a few more miles between us, I'll let you have that bath I promised you. I'll fix us a hot meal, something better than granola bars. Just hang in there a little bit longer. I'll get you out of this. I promise."

He squeezed her hand. Jessica squeezed his in return, but as she lay in the dark thinking about what he'd said, tension and dread coiled in her stomach. Ryan didn't normally bother to explain his actions. The fact that he had, meant they were probably in far greater danger than she'd realized.

She prayed that Ryan hadn't just made her another promise that he couldn't keep.

Chapter Ten

"Who's Miss Beth?"

Jessica jerked her head up. Ryan was sitting in the dirt a few feet away, skinning the rabbit he'd caught for breakfast, after making them hike a few more hours away from the cave where they'd slept last night. Jessica averted her gaze to keep from gagging. "Where did you hear that name?"

"You were talking in your sleep again."

Jessica raised her brows in question.

"Don't worry," Ryan said. "You didn't mention your bank account number, or your social security number, and you didn't reveal the names of any of your old boyfriends. The only words I understood were *Miss Beth*."

Jessica gave a short laugh. "You already know my bank account number, and my social security number. And that list of old boyfriends is pathetically short."

Ryan's face registered his surprise, reminding Jessica that he'd assumed she'd slept with DeGaullo.

He probably thought she'd slept with a host of men. She pursed her lips.

Ryan set the poor, dead rabbit on a rock. Grabbing one of the small branches he'd gathered earlier, he started trimming the end into a sharp point with the smaller of the two knives he had. "So, who's Miss Beth?" he repeated.

Jessica considered not answering, but she'd learned he wouldn't stop pestering her until he got what he wanted. "One of my many foster moms. One of the few who seemed to care about me."

Ryan's hand stilled for a moment. "Do you miss her?"

"Sometimes, maybe. She taught me how to cook." She grinned. "Or at least, she tried."

"I thought you cooked a great breakfast the other day."

"Sure. You like burned food. Right."

He grinned and held the twig up, examining the tip.

"She may have been a failure at teaching me to cook, but Miss Beth gave me my love for math. She also taught me how to drive. Although, I did tear up her clutch trying to learn to drive a stick shift."

"Remind me never to let you drive my Jeep," he teased. "How long were you in foster care?"

Too long. She looked out over the mountains and the endless acres of trees. She'd climbed many a tree when she was young, usually to get away from her foster-siblings and their cruel taunts. She'd never fit in, probably because she was always on edge, worried someone would find out about her parents.

Somehow, they always did.

"How long?" He repeated, studying her intently. The man definitely didn't know how to take a hint.

She sighed. "I think I was five, maybe six, when I went into foster care. I left on my eighteenth birthday, so…twelve or thirteen years, I guess."

His brows rose. "You were never adopted?"

She grabbed one of the twigs and poked at the ground. "It's pretty obvious that I came from bad stock, as one of my foster parents used to tell me. Otherwise, I wouldn't have turned out the way I did, right?" She hated how bitter she sounded, but Ryan had struck a nerve.

How many times had she gotten her hopes up when a new family considered her for adoption, only to have them change their mind and choose someone else when they found out about her biological parents? She sniffed, determined not to give in to the unwelcome wave of self-pity that shot through her.

But then the tears started flowing down her face, and Ryan lifted her onto his lap, cradling her in the warm cocoon of his arms.

She didn't question why he was being so nice. It felt so good to be held. It had been so long since someone had cared, or even pretended to care. She closed her eyes and clung to him, resting her cheek against his chest and taking the comfort he offered.

Neither of them spoke for a long time. When the tears dried on Jessica's face, Ryan gave her a gentle squeeze, but he continued to hold her.

"Tell me about your biological parents," he whispered against the top of her head.

"There's not much to tell. My mom was a junkie. She loved crack more than she loved me. And you already know my dad abandoned me. He was arrested, then went in and out of prison after that. Last I heard he was doing hard time for murder." She shrugged. "See, I told you I came from bad stock. People always expect the worst from me, and so far, they've been right."

And one of the worst offenders, the person who thought she was *almost* as bad as DeGaullo, was the man holding her.

She scrambled off his lap.

Ryan frowned, obviously wondering what had happened.

Jessica's stomach chose that moment to growl. Loudly.

Ryan grinned. "Even if you don't think you want some of this rabbit, your stomach obviously does." He reached for the stick he'd sharpened, grabbed the skinned rabbit, and skewered it like a corn dog at a fair.

Jessica's stomach heaved. She silently gave thanks that it was empty at the moment, and that she'd been born in the age of grocery stores and restaurants. She'd have never survived in pioneer days. "I'm not really all that hungry anymore," she said, fighting nausea.

"Be brave. You'll feel much better after a hot meal."

"I can't eat Thumper."

"Would you rather eat Bambi? I can try to find a deer if you prefer venison."

She grimaced and he grinned in response. He made a small ring of rocks next to one of the oak trees a few feet away and placed some twigs inside it. After shoving two Y-shaped sticks into the ground, he set the speared rabbit on top of them. With a quick flick of his lighter, the twigs lit and a small fire burned beneath the rabbit.

The smell of roasting meat hit Jessica, and her stomach clenched, this time with hunger instead of nausea. Her qualms about eating Thumper were rapidly disappearing. She tried to remember the last time she'd eaten a real meal, something other than a granola bar. It was probably the sandwiches she and Ryan had made for lunch while unpacking her garage a few days ago.

"Why did you build the fire under a tree?" She watched him feed small twigs to the flames, one at a time.

"Keeping the fire small, and using dry twigs, reduces the smoke. The tree leaves clean and obscure what little smoke there is."

"Did you learn that when you were an army ranger?"

"Actually, I learned that from my dad. He made sure all of us could handle pretty much anything. He took us camping out on the ranch dozens of times, teaching us survival skills. When I became a teenager, he took me camping for the first time without the rest of my family. It was kind of a rite of passage, a family tradition. I had to hunt for our meal, clean it and cook it. Basically I had to prove I could survive on my own, all without leaving any tracks so my other brothers and my sister couldn't find us."

"Why did it matter if they found you?"

"It was a game, to see who was the best, and to make sure all of us could take care of ourselves no matter what happened. He made sure we were strong, independent, so we never had to rely on anyone else. The ranch is huge. A kid could get lost out there for days. Dad wanted to make sure if that happened that each of his kids could find their way back home without getting hurt." He grinned. "He also taught us to avoid mountain lions, of course."

She lightly punched him in the arm. "So who was the best? You?"

"Nope. My sister. She beat me at every game we ever played."

The unguarded look of love in his eyes told Jessica that he didn't mind at all that his sister usually won. Part of her wondered if he let her win on purpose, just to make his sister happy. He obviously cared very much about his family, especially—it seemed—his sister and his mother.

That didn't surprise Jessica. She was beginning to realize he'd been brought up the old-fashioned way, to respect women and to be protective of them. That explained why he'd been so protective of her all along. Even though he made no secret of his disdain for her past and what she'd done, Ryan put her safety and comfort first.

Even back in the hospital, when his anger about his friends' deaths was so fresh and new, he'd gently unwound the IV tubing that had tangled around her arm and made sure she was comfortable. His need to protect was automatic, and sometimes in direct contrast to his emotions.

The fact that he was willing to defy his boss's orders and risk his career to keep her safe made more sense to her now. Protecting her wasn't a choice. It was something he felt he *had* to do, because she was a woman, and he believed she needed him.

It certainly wasn't because he was beginning to care about her. She sighed and drew a line in the dirt with one of the small twigs.

Ryan turned the rabbit and tested the meat with his knife.

"Would your sister eat rabbit in a situation like this?" Jessica asked.

He quirked a brow. "She would have caught,

skinned and cooked the rabbit the first time I offered her a granola bar."

Jessica laughed. "You love your family very much, don't you?"

"Of course." He looked surprised that she'd even said that. "They mean everything to me. *Family* means everything to me." His voice sounded matter-of-fact, as if he thought everyone felt that way.

Maybe they did. Jessica had never had a family, so she didn't know if Ryan was any different than other people in that respect. What she did know was that she envied him. She envied the love in his eyes and the pride in his voice when he talked about the games he and his siblings played.

The rabbit meat turned dark and began to sizzle. Jessica's mouth watered from the tantalizing smell.

Ryan cut off a small piece of cooked meat, and blew on it to cool it.

"Did you eat rabbits to survive when you were on your army missions?" Jessica asked.

"Not unless we ran out of rations, or we were deep in enemy territory and had no way of getting supplies through normal channels. On our last mission, we were more likely to eat lamb than rabbit."

"Lamb? They lived wild where you were?"

His lopsided smile did something funny to her stomach.

"Not exactly. Let's just say the world was our supermarket."

"You stole?" She was genuinely shocked.

"We were surrounded by unfriendlies. I couldn't exactly walk up to a farmer and offer him a couple of dollars for a lamb. We took what we needed. No one went hungry or lost their farms because of our pilfering." He held out the piece of rabbit meat toward her. "Come on, Jessie. I know you're hungry. Don't let Thumper's sacrifice be in vain."

Her breath caught at his unexpected use of the nickname she hadn't heard since college. Not even Natalie had called her Jessie, saying she was far too serious to be anything other than Jessica.

The last time she'd allowed herself to be Jessie, she'd been happy, naive, full of foolish hopes and dreams. Then she'd answered an ad in the paper, and her dreams became a nightmare.

"Jessica," Ryan said, his voice quiet, concerned. "What's wrong?"

She shook her head. "Nothing. I'm just hungry."

She reached out to take the piece of meat on his knife, but he took the meat and leaned forward, holding it against her mouth. When she opened her mouth to protest, he slid the food between her lips, his thumb brushing against her lower lip. She shivered at the unexpected caress. Then the wild, gamey taste of the rabbit burst across her tongue and she moaned in surprised delight.

"Oh, my gosh, this is so good."

"Better than a granola bar?" he teased. He cut another piece and blew on it.

She plucked it from his hand before he could feed her again. "Definitely better than a granola bar."

His nostrils flared and his gaze dipped down to her lips as she took a bite. She coughed to keep from choking when he licked his lips.

"You okay?" He pounded her on the back.

She ducked away from his hand. "I'm fine. Stop beating me."

He rolled his eyes and plopped a piece of rabbit into his mouth. When they were both finished eating, he disposed of the carcass and covered the fire with dirt. He started to slide the knife into his boot, but instead he reached out and took hold of one of her boots, tugging her foot toward him.

"Hey, what are you doing?"

"I don't have an extra gun to give you, but you should have something to defend yourself. Just in case." He made a slit in the stitching at the top of her boot and slid the knife inside. The handle stuck out just enough to grasp.

She reached down and pulled the knife out, then slid it back in. She was impressed at his handiwork, and humbled that he trusted her enough to give her a weapon. "Thank you."

"You're welcome." He climbed to his feet and tugged her up to stand with him. "Let's take that bath now." He grabbed the backpack and threw it over his shoulder, pulling her behind him.

If she'd still been eating, she would have choked when he gave her a slow, sexy wink.

The stream he took her to looked like a slice of heaven. Birds chirped in the trees overhead. The sunlight made the water sparkle like tiny diamonds as it gurgled over the rocks. Water sprayed into the air, creating an enchanting mist that gave the place an ethereal quality.

"It's beautiful," she said, her voice low and reverent.

"Breathtaking."

When she turned to look at him she realized he was looking at her instead of the stream. She tried to think of some sassy retort, but her brain seemed stuck in befuddled mode. Ryan took mercy on her and led her to a shallow part of the stream. The water was clear, no more than a foot deep.

He set the backpack on the dry bank, pulled out a change of clothes for himself, then one for her, along with shampoo and two bars of soap. "Will ten minutes be long enough?" he asked.

She nearly drooled when he handed her the shampoo. "I guess so. Where are you going?"

"To bathe. Unless you want me to stay here with you."

Her breath caught in her throat. Before she could figure out how to respond, Ryan winked again and disappeared into the trees.

Jessica stared after him, not sure what to think. But then she realized she'd already wasted one of those precious minutes he'd given her, so she hurriedly stripped.

The cold air had her shivering in no time, but she was too relieved to be out of her filthy clothes to care. The idea of submerging in a cold mountain stream was daunting, but she desperately wanted to be clean. Before she could talk herself out of it, she hurried into the water, sucking in her breath at how cold it was. Her teeth were chattering as she quickly lathered her hair.

She washed her clothes, too, and dunked her entire body in the frigid water, gasping in shock when she came up for air. Violent shivers shook her and her hands were numb by the time she was done. She grabbed her wet clothes and climbed out of the water. Without a towel to dry herself, she used her wet clothes to wipe the water from her skin.

Freezing to death seemed like a very real possibility right now. She dressed as quickly as she could in the extra shirt and jeans Ryan had given her, and put her jacket on. When the shivers became more bearable, she laid her old clothes out on some rocks in the sun to dry. She sat on another rock in the full sun, hoping her hair would dry soon, too, and trying to absorb some of the sun's heat.

"Are you decent?"

She jerked around at the sound of Ryan's voice, but she didn't see him anywhere. "I'm dressed."

A moment later he emerged from the cover of trees and sat next to her. He glanced at her wet hair before his gaze slid down her body, as if he could see everything hidden beneath her jacket. He seemed to tear his gaze away with effort before staring out over the water.

"Ryan, what's going on?" Jessica's frustration and confusion made her voice much harsher than she'd intended.

His face showed his surprise. "What do you mean?"

"Why are you acting as if you're attracted to me all of a sudden? And you're being so…nice. You haven't called me city girl all morning. Why not?"

His jaw tightened. "You don't like it when I'm a jerk. And you don't like it when I'm not a jerk. Tell me, Jessie. How do you want me to act? Just say the word and I'll do it."

Jessica curled her hands into fists. "Stop it. Stop using that cute pet name as if you care about me. I know you don't. You were quite clear about how you felt about me when we first met. Now you're flirting and acting like you…" She clamped her mouth shut, shaking her head.

Ryan's hair was wet, and a bead of water was slowly trickling down the side of his neck. Without stopping to think, Jessica reached out to wipe the drop of water away, but when her fingers touched his skin, he stiffened.

She snatched her hand back and jumped to her feet. "That's the Ryan I'm used to, the one whose skin crawls if I get too close. Welcome back." She turned and ran into the woods.

RYAN FOUGHT THE urge to call Jessica back. She needed a moment alone, and he needed the break just as much as she did. How could she have ever thought he was disgusted by her? Yes, he despised her past and the things she'd done, but he'd always wanted her. He'd lain awake most of the night, wanting her so much he'd finally decided to pursue her this morning, and let her know that he wanted her. Big mistake.

He grabbed a rock and threw it across the stream. He didn't *want* to want Jessica, and he certainly didn't want to care about her. But he couldn't seem to help it. With the childhood she'd had, she had every right to hate and resent everyone around her. And yet, she seemed to genuinely grieve and feel responsible for the marshals who'd lost their lives protecting her.

Ryan didn't know how he would have turned out if he'd grown up in the environment Jessica had. But part of him suspected he wouldn't have been anywhere near the person she was. She was right. He'd been judging her all along, and he shouldn't have.

Last night, her grateful declaration of thanks, for saving *someone like me,* had told him far more than she realized. Jessica didn't think she deserved to be saved. And how was she supposed to feel differently when people like him constantly reminded her of her past?

He sat staring out across the water for several more minutes, but the confusing thoughts inside his head wouldn't settle. And sitting here wasn't going to resolve anything. It certainly wasn't making Jessica any safer.

The terrain was getting so rough now that the motorcycle wasn't the advantage it had once been. Using the bike meant they could only travel safely during daylight hours, so he could see the obstacles in their path, and so the bike's headlights wouldn't attract any attention. The man following them had no such restrictions.

No matter how many times Ryan backtracked or left false trails, he still caught occasional glimpses of their pursuer through his binoculars. This morning was the first time he hadn't been able to locate the gunman, which had Ryan's danger radar going into overdrive. Whether he could see the man or not, Ryan knew he was still out there, getting closer all the time.

It was almost as if the gunman knew where Ryan was going.

Chapter Eleven

"We're out of gas." Ryan gave up trying to restart the motorcycle. He hopped off and held the bike steady for Jessica.

She had mixed feelings as she slid off the seat. They'd spent the past two days alternating between riding the bike and pushing it, because the woods were so full of rocks and fallen trees that riding the motorcycle was sometimes too dangerous.

Still, even though her legs were wobbly, her rear end was sore, and her lower back ached, she didn't relish the idea of walking the rest of the way to wherever they were going.

"Don't motorcycles get, like, a hundred miles to the gallon or something?" She nudged one of the tires with her boot.

"Not quite. But the tank wasn't full, anyway. I had it drained before the Feds shipped it up here. The gas can I used to fill the tank the morning of the fire was only half full."

"This is your motorcycle? I assumed the government leased you a motorcycle to use while you were up here, just like they leased me a car."

"It's mine." His sigh sounded closer to a groan.

Jessica clucked her tongue in sympathy. "As far as we've gone, there has to be a road close around here somewhere. Can't we just push the bike a little farther until we get to a gas station?"

"Oh, sure. I think there's one right next to the Walmart around the corner."

Jessica narrowed her eyes at him. "Throw in a smart remark about bears and I'll kick you."

Ryan opened his mouth to speak.

"In the groin," Jessica promised.

He clamped his mouth shut.

"Okay." Jessica tapped her hand against her thigh. "So, we ditch the bike…"

A pained expression crossed Ryan's face. "I suppose I can hide it and come back for it later."

Jessica cocked her head and studied the bike. She didn't notice anything particularly special about it. It wasn't all that big. It wasn't even a pretty color. Red would have been nice, or maybe even blue, but it was black. Mostly chrome, with a little black paint thrown in like an afterthought.

"So, ah, what kind is it?"

"Harley-Davidson Nightrod." Ryan's voice held a note of reverence as if he were in church. "Twelve-fifty cc, multivalve, fuel-injected engine. It's a crime to treat her the way I have, taking her off-road, bumping around on the trails."

"Your bike is a female?"

He cocked a brow. "I could *so* make you blush right now, but I'll take the high road."

Her face flushed hot, anyway. "Are we taking the bike with us or not?"

"We'll leave the bike. Just give me a minute." He walked the motorcycle a few feet away and laid it against a tree.

"When I called Stuart this morning," he said, as he turned back to her, "he told me about a forest ranger cabin not far from here. We might still be able to make it before nightfall if we hurry. I'm sure you'd enjoy sleeping in a real bed for a change."

The cabin sounded like heaven, but Jessica couldn't resist teasing him one last time. "I don't know." She waved her hand toward the bike. "Are you sure you can leave her behind? What if she gets lonely?"

"I don't suppose anyone has ever accused you of being a smart-ass."

"Why? Are you calling me one?"

He rolled his eyes. "Wouldn't dream of it."

Ryan started hiking at a fast pace, making Jessica pant to keep up with him. She vowed if she ever got back to civilization again, she'd thank her Zumba instructor for pushing her so hard back when she used to take a formal exercise class. She'd kept up her exercise routines even back in the safe house, so she was in pretty good condition, but she was still struggling to keep up.

Ryan took mercy on her, slowing down until they fell into a stride that suited them both. Jessica was even more grateful now for the hiking boots Ryan had given her. She was still blister free, and her feet were toasty warm.

When the path widened enough for them to jog side by side, Ryan slowed to a walk to let Jessica rest. He took advantage of the downtime to teach her how to leave as few tracks as possible. He showed her the best places to step, to look for the harder surfaces and stay out of the dirt. He taught her to backtrack to confuse anyone following them. And he showed her how to be whisper quiet, avoiding dry leaves or twigs that would snap and give away her presence.

He asked her questions about her past, about growing up in foster care. He asked her about her college days, and seemed surprised when she spoke about her volunteer work with special-needs children.

"What made you want to work with the kids?" he asked.

She frowned and thought about it. "I'm not sure. I guess, maybe, because I could kind of identify with what they were going through. I knew how it felt to be picked on, or for other people to assume things about you, all because of something beyond your control."

"You mean, because of your parents?"

"Yes. I didn't choose to have bad parents, but

I had to live with the stigma of what they'd done. Those kids didn't have a choice, either." She glanced away, feeling uncomfortable with him staring at her as if he was trying to figure her out. "Heck, I probably did it more for me than them. They gave me something I'd never had before, something I'd craved for so long."

"What was that?"

"Unconditional love," she whispered, her throat tightening. She took off in a jog, hoping the cool air against her face and the exercise would help her get her emotions back under control again. The longer she was around Ryan, the more she seemed to open up about her past and the more emotional she was getting.

Ryan easily caught up to her and jogged beside her in silence for a while. When he spoke again, he didn't ask her more questions. Instead, he shared stories about his own past, entertaining her with tales about the many pranks one of his brothers liked to pull on some of their cousins.

Soon Jessica was laughing right along with him. She sighed wistfully. "I think I'd like your family. Just how many cousins and aunts and uncles do you have?"

He pressed his lips together as if deep in thought. "Don't know," he finally said. "A lot. Our family reunions usually fill an entire floor of the Motel 6 down the street."

She gave him a droll look. "Motel 6?"

"Kidding." He winked.

She shook her head. "What was it like growing up on a ranch? Did you grow corn, or tobacco or what?"

"Now *you're* kidding, right?"

"No, why?"

"It was a horse ranch, not a farm. We bred horses. Still do. A lot of work, but rewarding, especially during the summer when my parents host camps for troubled teens. My mom calls it horse therapy. My dad calls it tough love. He believes that giving a kid responsibility and making him work hard will make him a better person, and make him appreciate what he has."

She was surprised to find out they both had something in common in their past. "Sounds like you enjoyed working with kids, too. Kids who needed you."

"I did. Still do. I always take a few weeks off every summer to go back and help out with the camps. I go home every Christmas, too." He grinned. "For the Motel 6 reunion."

"I've always wanted a family, a big family," she said wistfully. "But that will never happen."

"Why not? You can make your own family."

She shook her head at that nonsense, ruthlessly squelching the longing that sprang up inside her at his words. "I couldn't bear putting a family in danger, always fearing DeGaullo might find me someday and hurt the ones I love."

Ryan glanced at her sharply. He fell silent as he jogged beside her.

A few minutes later, Jessica slowed to a walk and Ryan slowed along with her.

"I'm hungry." Jessica tried for a lighthearted tone, desperate to break the tension that had settled over both of them. She wiggled her nose in an imitation of a rabbit. "Got any more of that yummy Thumper in your backpack?"

He smiled. "Ah, no. Fresh out, sorry. How about a granola bar, instead?"

"Yum!" She rubbed her tummy, and they both laughed.

It was late afternoon when Ryan called a halt for their dinner break. Jessica collapsed on the ground beside a tree while Ryan dug out the usual granola bars and water.

"When can we have another rabbit?" she grumbled as she took a bite of her granola bar.

"Haven't seen any. How adventurous are you?"

She glanced at him suspiciously. "Why?"

"Ever eaten squirrel?"

"No. And I'm not going to. I don't eat rats, either, which is basically what a squirrel is. I'll stick to the granola bars, thank you very much. How many more do we have?"

"Enough for one more day, if I don't catch us something before then. I promise I won't let you starve."

"How much longer do you think we'll have to hide out?"

"Hard to say. I'll call my boss once we reach the cabin, see how the investigation is going. This deep into the mountains, the cabin should be self-contained. It will have a propane tank, and a fresh-water well, which means you'll have plenty of hot water for a shower."

A flare of excitement shot through Jessica at the mention of a shower, but it wasn't enough to help her keep her tired eyes open. She fell asleep dreaming of fluffy towels and soft beds.

JESSICA WAS WARM all over, cozier than she'd been in days. She snuggled against the source of the warmth, yawned, opened her eyes…and looked directly into Ryan's deep blue ones.

He was leaning back against a tree and she was sitting in his lap, facing him.

Heat flushed through her from the top of her head to the tips of her toes. She gave an awkward laugh, not quite sure how to extricate herself without making the situation even more embarrassing. "What did I do, fall asleep and crawl onto your lap?"

"I picked you up. You were shivering."

"Oh. Well, thanks. I think." Her face flamed as she thought about Ryan scooping her up while she was sleeping and settling her in his lap.

She put her hands on his shoulders and pushed herself up, but he grabbed her waist, holding her still.

"You don't have to go." His voice was a deep, sexy whisper.

Jessica froze. Ryan reached out and swept her hair back from her face. The naked hunger in his eyes was undeniable this time. Her belly tightened in response.

He must have seen her answering hunger, because his eyelids went to half-mast and he slowly bent his head toward her.

He was going to kiss her. Jessica had wanted this for so long. She didn't know why he wanted to kiss her now, but she was eager to feel his lips on hers, to see if he tasted as good as he did in her dreams. She put her arms around him and leaned forward, angling her lips toward his, breathing in his intoxicating scent.

His eyes widened and he looked over her shoulder.

"Ah, hell."

She blinked in surprise. He stood in one fluid motion, lifting her up toward the branch hanging over them.

"What are you doing?" She clutched at the branch to keep from falling.

"Climb, Jessica. Climb!"

Chapter Twelve

Black bears were supposed to be nonaggressive and shy around humans. Apparently, no one had explained that to the bear that charged out of the bushes. After Ryan boosted Jessica onto the branch, she fairly flew up the oak tree, rediscovering her childhood tree-climbing skills.

Unfortunately, her flight up the tree wasn't necessary. Ryan easily scared the bear away by yelling and waving his arms. As quickly as the bear had appeared, it was gone. Now Jessica was standing on a branch halfway up the tree with her arms wrapped around the trunk, trying to climb back down.

She suspected the task would be easier if she could gather the courage to actually move. A gust of wind shook the branch she was standing on and she squealed, tightening her hold.

"Do you need help?" Ryan called out from below.

"I'll have you know I was a champion tree climber in my youth. I could out-climb all the other foster kids, even the boys. I can get down by myself."

"If you say so."

"Ryan, are you laughing at me?"

"Wouldn't dream of it."

She gritted her teeth and edged her foot to the next branch. "*Sugar.* I can't believe I climbed so high. What was I thinking?" she grumbled.

"Did you say something, Jessie?"

"No," she lied.

"Okay."

Even from high up in the tree she could hear the laughter in his voice. She gritted her teeth and tried to gather her courage to lower herself to the next branch.

In the end, Ryan had to come up and get her. He blanketed his body around her, giving her the feeling of security she needed to lower one arm at a time, one foot at a time. Before long, she was sitting next to him on a tree stump, pretending her shivers were from the cold and not because she was still recovering from her scare. He handed her a bottle of water and took one for himself.

She warily eyed the bushes across from them. "Will the bear come back?"

"Probably. But not while we're still here. The only reason she ran at us was because we startled her and she felt cornered."

"She?"

"I'm guessing, based on her size. The females are smaller than the males. You did a great job climbing that tree, by the way. Impressive."

"Yeah, an impressive display of cowardice. I'm good at running away from danger."

"You are not a coward." Each word was pronounced slowly, forcefully, as he stared into her eyes. "You testified against a powerful man, knowing the risks and the costs. Not many people would have done that. The only reason DeGaullo is still a free man is because those jurors didn't have the courage you have."

Jessica stared at him in shock. Those were words she'd never expected to hear from U.S. Marshal Ryan Jackson. "Thank you."

"You're welcome." He took a sip from his bottle of water. "There is one thing that puzzles me, though."

"What's that?"

"I don't understand how you got mixed up with him in the first place. You're a smart woman. What happened?"

She tightened the cap on her water bottle with short, jerky movements, unable to hide her irritation. She wasn't sure who she was irritated with more, though—Ryan, for asking the question, or herself for all the mistakes she'd made.

"I'm sure the Justice Department has a thick file on me. Didn't they let you read it?"

"I read what I was given, which was mostly about DeGaullo and his guns for hire so that I'd recognize them if I ever saw them. Most of what I know, I read in the papers. I know you took a job for De-

Gaullo's accounting firm fresh out of college, and that you worked for him for five years."

Some of Jessica's anger faded. Anyone relying on the newspapers for their facts wouldn't have known half the details. "I didn't *know* DeGaullo owned the firm when I took that job."

"When did you find out?" He sounded surprised.

"Three or four years later. DeGaullo has a lot of legitimate businesses, you know, buried under a web of corporations that own other corporations. I worked on the accounts for several of those businesses, with no reason to suspect anything was wrong."

"You can't tell me you didn't help DeGaullo launder money. That's the basis of the case against him—your records and your testimony."

"Really?" She raised a brow. "Are you sure about that?"

"Am I wrong?"

She frowned at him. "Yes and no. Once I was entrenched in his legitimate businesses, I was gradually brought in to help on others. When I saw DeGaullo's name on some of those accounts, I spoke to one of the other women about it."

"Natalie, the woman who died?"

She clenched her fists in her lap. "Yes. She was my best friend, my only friend, really. When I started asking questions, she pulled me aside and told me what was going on. She told me about other accountants who used to work there, people who had disappeared when they started asking questions. I was so scared that I called in sick two days in a row, trying to figure out what to do."

"You went to the FBI."

"No, not that time. If I had, I would be dead right now. Natalie told me all about it, that DeGaullo had us followed and he'd kill us if we ever told anyone about his finances. I sat in the dark those two nights after calling in sick and watched the street outside my apartment. It didn't take long to realize she was right. There was always someone there, watching. I'd never had a reason to suspect anything before, but when I saw someone outside, I knew she was right."

"After that, you just went back to work for him, cooking the books?"

She started to get up, but he grabbed her hand.

"I want to understand."

Jessica frowned at him. "Yes, I cooked the books for another year after finding out who I was really working for. Are we done now?"

She tried to pull away from him, but again he wouldn't let her go. Instead, he pulled her onto his lap and tightened his arms around her.

"We are far from done. Tell me the rest."

Jessica stiffened at the thread of steel underlying his voice. "Why?"

"Because I deserve to know the facts about the woman I jumped into a burning building to save."

"That's not fair."

"Life's not fair."

She blew out a breath in frustration. "There isn't much more to tell. Natalie dragged me back to work, insisting I wouldn't be safe unless I got back to my normal routine. She was right. De-Gaullo's men watched me much more closely after those sick days. It was a long time before they relaxed their guard. That's when I finally contacted the FBI. They were excited to have someone on the inside. They had me gather evidence against him for months. The night Natalie died, the Feds had told me to get out. DeGaullo had discovered that someone on the inside was leaking information. He knew it was one of his accountants, but he wasn't sure who. I was grabbing the last of the evidence the Feds needed when I heard him outside the office."

Ryan tightened his arms around her. "Go on."

"I warned Natalie to hide, but I didn't have time to explain. She thought I was silly to hide under my desk. I never told her I was working for the FBI, so she didn't realize why DeGaullo was there. We weren't supposed to be there after hours. I think when he saw her he assumed she was the one who'd leaked the information. He didn't even give her a chance to talk. He just…shot her."

She shivered and Ryan drew her close, kissing the top of her head. "You were lucky he didn't see you."

"I really don't want to talk about this anymore." She scrambled off his lap and took off jogging down the trail.

JESSICA WAS GRATEFUL that Ryan didn't try to press her any further, or ask her more questions. He silently jogged behind her, and gave her the time she needed to calm down.

When the trail ended at a rock wall, he took her hand and quietly led her back through the woods to where the trees were much thinner, creating a wide expansive clearing with trees on one side and rocks on the other.

Jessica was so pleased to be out of the gloomy woods for a change, with the warm sun shining down on her face, that she didn't even mind when Ryan started walking beside her. A few minutes later, he surprised her by putting his arm around her shoulders and hauling her roughly against him.

"Uh, Ryan, what are you doing?"

He rubbed her back and leaned down next to her ear. "Smile, Jessie. Pretend you want me."

Pretend? Not necessary. As soon as he'd put his arm around her shoulders she couldn't seem to draw in a normal breath.

Afraid he'd feel her heart thundering and know what he was doing to her, she tried to push his arm off her shoulder. "What are you doing? I don't under—"

He stopped and pulled her against him, capturing her lips with his in a searing kiss. She was so shocked, she was just starting to respond when he raised his head. Instead of pulling away from her, he trailed his hot mouth across her cheek next to her ear.

"Wrap your legs around me."

A wave of desire slammed into Jessica at his intimate suggestion, making her hot all over. When Ryan lifted her, pressing his hands beneath her bottom, she eagerly wrapped her legs around his waist. She moaned at the feel of his warm mouth against her neck.

"Ryan, what are you doing? This is crazy."

He pressed another soft kiss on her neck. "There's a man with a rifle trained on us fifty yards away."

She jerked in his arms but he held her so tightly she couldn't pull back.

"The only reason he isn't shooting is because we're giving him a show. Let's not disappoint him."

He started walking with her wrapped in his arms. Jessica gasped when he sucked on her neck. The feel of him hardening against her had her pulse pounding in her ears. "Ryan, stop this." She fought her instinctive need to rub her body against his. Someone was trying to kill them. Ryan needed to stop the madness so they could run.

"We're almost to the trees." He undulated his hips and lightly bit her earlobe.

She didn't have to fake the excitement that made her arch against him.

Ryan's breath quickened. "Careful, Jessie. I might want to finish this later."

His words had her arching against him again,

so turned on that she almost didn't care about the gunman. "Promises, promises." She nipped his earlobe in retaliation for the torture he was putting her through.

His knees buckled and he almost went down. He regained his footing, and his lips curved against her neck. "I'll pay you back for that later. When we get to the trees, I'm going to give you my gun. Don't run. Hunker down in one spot and be as quiet as you can, just like I taught you."

He did that sinful movement with his hips again. Jessica squeezed her legs around him.

He growled low in his throat. Then he was lunging into the trees with her wrapped tightly in his arms. A shot rang out and tree bark exploded next to them.

The gunman shouted behind them. Seconds later, shoes crunched on dry leaves and twigs as he ran after them.

Ryan shoved Jessica down behind a thick bush and thrust his gun into her hand. He pitched the backpack on the ground next to her.

"Keep your gun," Jessica whispered furiously.

Ryan ignored her and ran back to the path. He dove into the trees to avoid the next shot.

Jessica had to clamp her hand over her mouth to keep from shouting at him. Ryan was making himself a target to draw the gunman away from her. *Sugar!* If Ryan survived, she'd kill him herself for taking these kinds of chances.

RYAN CRASHED THROUGH the underbrush, purposely making noise to draw the gunman away from Jessica. The gunman took the bait, running after him like a sprinter in a marathon, taking wild shots with his rifle that ricocheted off trees and didn't come close to hitting their mark.

When they were both far enough away from Jessica to ensure her safety, Ryan changed tactics.

He stopped running.

He melted into the trees to wait for his prey. Just before the gunman got close enough for Ryan to pounce, the gunman skidded to a stop and brought up his rifle. He looked around wildly as if he'd only just realized he couldn't hear Ryan anymore.

A bird shrieked at the interruption in its routine. The gunman swung his rifle toward the sound. Ryan dove for cover as a wild shot rang out and struck the ground just inches from where he'd been standing.

The gunman raised his rifle. But Ryan had already thrown his knife. The gunman let out a grunt of pain and grabbed the hilt of the knife buried in his shoulder. Ryan lunged at him, but the gunman dove out of the way. He grabbed for his rifle where it had fallen, but Ryan reached the gun first.

The other man took off before Ryan could take a shot.

Ryan took off after him. When his quarry's trail turned toward a sheer drop-off down the side of the mountain, Ryan took advantage of the man's mistake and turned to cut him off where the trail would force him to turn back in Ryan's direction.

A few minutes later, Ryan was rewarded by the sight of the gunman, now carrying the knife that had been in his shoulder, jogging through the trees. Ryan timed the man's footfalls. Then he dropped down out of a tree and tackled the man to the forest floor. The man fell hard, cracking his head against the rock-strewn ground.

Ryan cursed his luck. The gunman wasn't going to get up again, ever. So much for getting any information out of him. Ryan turned the man's face toward him and took a long look. He wasn't a marshal, at least not one Ryan had met, which was a relief. He hated to think one of the men he worked with every day had turned traitor.

Not that it would be the first time.

Ryan retrieved his knife and wiped it clean on the dead man's shirt before shoving it into his belt. He checked the rifle. Empty. A thorough check of the man's pockets didn't reveal any extra ammunition. The man must have assumed he wouldn't need to reload and he'd left his extra ammo with his supplies. He certainly didn't have any supplies on him, and he couldn't survive up in these mountains for long without supplies.

Without knowing where the bullets were stored, the rifle was useless. Ryan tossed it aside.

The gunman didn't have a wallet, no ID. He wasn't wearing a ring, even though there was a white circle around his ring finger to indicate he normally wore one. Ryan couldn't imagine one of DeGaullo's thugs worrying about carrying identifying information. So who was he?

He snapped the battery in his phone and took a picture of the dead man's face. He sent the photo to Stuart with a message to try to find out who the man was. Then Ryan disabled his phone again.

He'd left Jessica alone far longer than he'd intended. If this gunman had found them, there could be others. A growing sense of urgency had him pumping his arms and legs, sprinting down the trail, praying he hadn't made a horrible mistake by leaving Jessica alone.

Chapter Thirteen

The sound of gunshots galvanized Jessica into action. She wasn't about to sit and hide when someone was shooting at Ryan and he didn't have a gun to defend himself.

She took off running in the direction Ryan had gone. About twenty minutes later, she kicked the pile of leaves and pinecones in front of her and plopped down on the same fallen pine tree she'd already passed.

Three times.

Ryan had shown her how to not leave a trail, but he'd never bothered to show her how to follow someone else's trail. That was the first lesson she'd insist on once she caught up to him. Of course, that would come only after she yelled at him for giving her his gun and facing down a man with a rifle.

A bug flitted past her ear and she swatted it away. When another bug buzzed in front of her face, she jumped up and headed in what she hoped was a new direction, one that wouldn't send her in a circle again.

"Jessica."

Relief swamped her at the sound of Ryan's deep voice behind her. She turned around, and barely had time to register the anxious look on his face before he grabbed her arm and towed her behind him.

He took off at a fast jog. Jessica struggled to keep up with his long stride. When she tried to ask him why they were running, he hissed for her to be quiet. A few minutes later they reached the place where he'd originally left her. He leaned down and grabbed the backpack and shrugged it on.

"Gun?" he asked, holding out his hand.

She handed it to him, surprised that she'd actually forgotten she was holding it. "What's wrong? What happened back there?" She chewed her bottom lip and glanced back toward where they'd just come from. "Is the gunman still after us?"

"No, but we have to get moving in case there are others, in case anyone heard the shots. Remember what I taught you about being quiet, and leaving no trail?"

"Yes," she whispered, automatically lowering her voice to match his.

He grabbed her hand and took off running again, practically dragging her behind him.

THEY RAN UNTIL Jessica's side hurt so much she couldn't run anymore. She'd barely recovered when Ryan grabbed her hand, and took off running again. He repeated that cycle twice more. The last time, impatient with how long Jessica was taking to recover from the most recent jaunt, Ryan scooped her up and threw her over his shoulder to keep her moving.

He refused to answer any questions and demanded her silence. His anxiety and sense of urgency had her anxiously watching the forest around them just as intently as he was.

She gasped for breath, almost wishing their pursuers would find them and put her out of her misery, when Ryan finally called a halt to their mad dash through the forest.

Jessica plopped down right where she was and lay spread-eagled on the ground. Her chest heaved, her pulse pounded in her ears, and she was so nauseated she abruptly sat up and started gagging.

Ryan was immediately beside her, holding her hair out of her face as she dry heaved. There was nothing to throw up, but her body took a while to realize that before she stopped heaving.

She shoved her hair away from her face with a shaky hand and leaned back against a tree.

"I'm sorry, Jessie. I pushed you too hard. You're dehydrated, and you need to eat." Ryan handed her a bottle of water, and a granola bar.

Knowing they were running low on granola bars, Jessica broke it in two, refusing to eat any of it until Ryan grudgingly took the other half.

Several minutes later, when the nausea settled down and she felt human again, she climbed to her feet. She winced. The mad dash had earned her a set of blisters.

"What happened back there with the gunman?" she asked. "Why did we just run a marathon?"

"The gunman is dead. I wasn't sure if he was alone, so I wanted to get us as far away from there as we could."

Jessica glanced around. "Do you think we're safe here?"

"For now, yes. You did a good job being quiet, keeping to the hard ground, not leaving a trail to follow."

Jessica blushed with pleasure, which seemed ridiculous when she thought about it. Who would have thought she'd ever be proud to be able to pass through the woods without leaving a trail? Like that was a skill she'd ever thought she'd need.

Ryan's face tightened into lines of disapproval as he stepped closer to her. "Why didn't you stay where I'd left you when I went after the gunman?"

"I was worried about you. I heard shots and thought you might need my help."

His face paled. "You went looking for me?" His hand shook as he ran it through his hair. "You could have been shot. That gunman was firing so wildly, he could have hit you." He cursed and glared at her. "Don't go running after me if I'm chasing someone with a gun. You got that?"

By the time he finished his tirade he was glaring down at her.

That was it. She'd followed his orders all day and had the blisters to prove it. She wasn't putting up with any more orders today, or lectures. She jabbed her finger against his chest. "Taylor Hunt." She jabbed him again. "William Gavin. Joey Acres. Michael Rogers. Those are the four marshals who died protecting me. I don't want your name branded into my conscience, too. I don't want you to die for me."

His face had gone pale at the mention of the first name. He stared at her, his eyes wide. "You remember their names?"

"Of course I do. Why wouldn't I?" She whirled around and stomped through the bushes, struggling to hold back the angry words she wanted to say. For the first time since she'd testified against Richard DeGaullo, she'd gone on the offensive, determined to protect Ryan in any way she could. For what? So he could lecture her?

"Jessie, wait."

He caught up to her and grasped her shoulders. He forced her to turn around but she refused to look up at him.

"When I couldn't find you, I thought someone had…" His words faded away and he pulled her tightly against his chest.

He was worried about her? That's why he was so angry?

He gently pushed her back and cupped her face between his hands. "Don't *ever* scare me like that again." He yanked her toward him and captured her lips in a fierce kiss. When he stepped back, sympathy was etched on his face. "I'm so sorry to do this, but we have to keep going if we're going to make that cabin by nightfall."

The words he didn't say hung in the air between them. If one gunman had caught up to them, another one probably wasn't far behind. That's what he was really worried about. They had to keep moving.

Their lives depended on it.

"ARE YOU SURE a forest ranger isn't going to find us here?" Jessica asked, following Ryan into the cabin.

He smiled. "I think I can handle a park ranger if one drops by. There's a propane tank out back and I just flipped on the water heater. You'll have plenty of hot water for a shower in a few minutes. Go ahead and grab your clothes and scout around for a towel. I'll see if they've got anything in the pantry we can eat. Unless you prefer I hunt up a squirrel and make some stew."

She shuddered at the squirrel reference and he grinned back at her.

"What about heat?" she said, hoping she wouldn't have to put her jacket back on after taking a shower.

"If the fireplace was wood-burning, you'd be out of luck. But it's gas so we won't have to worry about the smoke alerting anyone. Go ahead and take your shower. By the time you're done it will be warm in here and I'll have something ready for us to eat."

"Every woman's dream. A hot guy who does all the cooking." Jessica's face flushed as soon as the words left her mouth. She grabbed her clothes and toiletries from the backpack and escaped into the bathroom.

RYAN GRINNED WHEN Jessica slammed the bathroom door. She flustered so easily. He loved the way her blush turned her fair skin a tantalizing pink. His mouth watered as he pictured how far down that pretty little blush extended.

His gaze drifted toward the bed that dominated the room. His pulse leaped at the thought of sharing it with her. He tamped down his raging desires with difficulty. There wasn't time for that nonsense. Jessica needed her sleep. She was exhausted. It was the only reason he'd taken the risk of staying in the cabin, and they couldn't stay for more than a few hours. Anything longer would be too risky without knowing how close their pursuers might be.

Or who, exactly, their pursuers were.

He snapped the battery into his cell phone. The first call he placed was to his boss. As usual, Alex answered on the first ring, and this time he recognized Ryan's number.

"Ryan, where are you? I've called a dozen times. Why didn't you bring the witness in—"

"Who torched Jessica's house?"

"What? Why are you ask—"

"I'm about to hang up."

"Wait, wait. Okay. I don't know for sure who's behind the fire yet, but I do have some new information. The police found the real Mike Higgins today, the insurance salesman, murdered in the woods. But we still don't know who the gunmen were that tried to kill you at your cabin."

"Do you have any leads at all?"

"Only a handful of people have access to the information on witness locations. We're looking at each of them, eliminating them one by one."

Ryan glanced at his watch. He was pushing his luck. Alex had to be trying to trace his phone right now. "The day of the courthouse bombing, you ordered me to fill in for Marshal Cole. Why?"

"Why? Cole was sick. The mistrial was declared unexpectedly. You still don't trust me, do you?"

"I gave my trust to a man I worked with for over two years in Afghanistan. He betrayed me and four of my men died. I've known you for far less time than that. So don't expect me to trust you, especially since you broke standard procedure on this case. Why did you assign me to move in next door to Jessica, and order me to stay—indefinitely? As far as I know, that's never been done before in WitSec."

Alex swore a blue streak. "Assigning you to stay with her wasn't my idea. It came down from my boss. When I questioned him about it—and I did ask—he said the order came from higher up, some suit in Washington. He thought it was because her case was so high profile, that we couldn't risk anything happening." He laughed harshly into the phone. "Fat lot of good that did."

Ryan winced. He'd deserved that, he supposed, if he looked at it from his boss's perspective. Still, he'd had to be sure. His gut told him his boss wasn't lying. "What's the name of that higher-up?"

Alex gave him the name, Alan Rivers, but it didn't sound familiar.

"Do you have trackers on our trail right now?"

"You know I do. They started out as soon as your twenty-four hours were up. You're neck deep in trouble for not bringing the witness in. I'm doing everything I can to find you two."

He glanced at his watch, nervous about being on the phone so long. He crossed to one of the two windows in the cabin and pulled the room-darkening curtain to the side to look out. "A gunman caught up to us today. There must be others out here, too. I doubt he was working alone."

"Since you're still breathing, can I assume he isn't?"

"He's no longer a threat."

Alex sighed. "Did you recognize him?"

"No." He thought about emailing his boss the picture on his phone, but he still wasn't sure he could trust him.

"Tell me where you are. I can get a helicopter out there, evac you out."

"Not until you find the mole."

He disconnected the call and made one more.

"Hello?"

"Stuart, it's Ryan. Did you get the photo I sent you?"

"Yeah, but I don't know who he is. Must be one of DeGaullo's low-level thugs."

"Maybe, I'm not sure. I also have a name for you to check out—Alan Rivers." When Stuart didn't answer, Ryan glanced at the phone to make sure the call hadn't been disconnected. "Stuart? You still there?"

"I'm here. Sorry. What was that name you wanted me to check—some guy named Rivers?"

"Alan Rivers, some Washington bureaucrat who passed down orders to my boss that went against WitSec's standard operating procedures. It's not much to go on, but it's something to look at. Have you gotten anywhere with your investigation?"

"Not much. Don't worry. We'll figure this out. I'll look into this Rivers guy. Where are you now?"

"In that cabin you told me about. I can't keep Jessica on this mountain anymore. It's too dangerous. I need a favor."

Chapter Fourteen

When Jessica opened the bathroom door she was delighted to see a roaring fire in the fireplace. The cabin was toasty warm and a mouthwatering smell came from the kitchenette where Ryan stood with his back to her.

She padded to him on bare feet, her toes curling against the cool, hardwood floor. He was stirring something with a long wooden spoon.

"Smells wonderful. What is it?"

"Would you believe beef stew?"

"Probably not."

He held a spoonful of the stew beneath her nose and her stomach growled at the incredible aroma.

"Please tell me it's not squirrel," she said.

"It's not squirrel."

She chewed her bottom lip. "You're not going to tell me it's Bambi, are you?"

His mouth quirked up in that familiar lop-sided grin. "Wouldn't dream of it."

It wasn't exactly a "no" but she was so hungry

she decided not to press. She wanted that stew. Desperately. "I don't suppose those forest rangers hid a Venti Mocha in their cupboard, did they?"

"I did see a pile of used Starbucks cups in the trash. I guess they drank it all."

"Selfish jerks. Okay, serve me up some of that squirrel stew. I'm starving."

"It's not squirrel. It came from a can."

Her stomach rumbled in answer. "Trust me. Right now I really don't care what it is."

Since there wasn't any furniture besides the bed, they both sat on the edge of the bed to eat. While Ryan took a shower, Jessica cleaned their dishes and replaced them in the pantry. She refilled their empty water bottles from the faucet and hand-washed their dirty clothes, hanging them on the countertops and stove handle to dry.

With nothing else to do, she stripped down to her T-shirt, turned down the comforter, and slid under the covers. The shower had turned off several minutes ago and she twisted her fingers in the sheets waiting for Ryan to come out.

Why was she so nervous? Except for the requisite bathroom breaks and hurried baths in freezing mountain streams, she and Ryan had been in each other's company constantly for days. So, they were going to share a bed tonight. It wasn't any different than sleeping on a pine bed in a cave, or at least it shouldn't be.

The bathroom door opened and Ryan stepped out

with a towel slung low on his hips. Jessica closed her mouth when she realized it had fallen open. She clutched the covers over her T-shirt, hungrily watching Ryan cross the room, his golden skin glowing in the firelight.

He double-checked the curtains, she presumed to make sure the light from the fireplace couldn't be seen from outside. Then he tucked his gun under the pillow next to her. He lifted the comforter to get into the bed, but paused when his gaze met hers. "Do you want me to sleep on the floor?"

"No, of course not. We've slept together this whole time. There's no reason for me to be shy."

"But you are. You're embarrassed. Your face is fire red." His gaze dipped down to her chest and she automatically raised the sheet, causing him to look back up into her eyes.

"Sleeping together in a real bed just seems...different somehow. You must think I'm a total prude." She fisted her hands in the comforter.

"I think you're refreshing."

She glanced away, uncomfortable with his praise since she'd been lusting after him from the day they'd met. She wanted him more now than ever. After the way he'd responded to her when they were giving the gunman *a show,* she'd taken it for granted that he wanted her, too. And yet, here he was offering to sleep on the floor. She didn't understand him. "Well, good night."

He slid under the covers and turned to face the other direction. "Night."

JESSICA WOKE UP blinking and glancing at the window next to the bed. The curtains were so heavy she couldn't tell if it was day or night outside. She started to reach for the curtain to look out.

"It's still dark outside, if that's what you're wondering."

She jerked around at the sound of Ryan's voice. He was sitting on the floor next to the fireplace with his back braced against the wall. Watching her.

"Ryan? Is something wrong?"

"We'll have to leave soon. Go back to sleep while you still can." His voice was deeper than usual, oddly strained. "Nothing's wrong."

"Then why are you sitting on the floor?"

He gave a short bark of laughter, his voice sounding harsh in the silence of the cabin. "You haven't dated much, have you?"

"Why would you ask me that?"

"Because you asked me why I'm sitting on the floor."

"I've dated. I'm not a virgin, you know." If her face got any hotter, she thought she'd die.

"And yet you have no idea why I'm sitting here instead of in bed? With you?"

Enlightenment dawned and her gaze flew toward his lap. His shorts did little to conceal his aroused state. He sighed and raised his right knee, shielding her view.

"Ryan, you confuse me."

"It's not that complicated. I'm a man. You're a beautiful woman."

"No. I'm not. That's what's confusing."

He stood in one fluid motion and approached the bed. He sat on the edge looking down at her, his brows drawn into a dark frown. "You *are* beautiful. Why is that so hard to accept?"

"I'm a geek, a nerd. Men, especially men like you, never pay attention to me."

"Men like me?"

She smoothed imaginary wrinkles from the sheet.

His hand covered hers, stilling her movements. "Men like me?" he repeated.

"Oh, come on. You're gorgeous. You could be a cover model for a fashion magazine if it weren't for all your muscles."

The corner of his mouth quirked up in a wry grin. "I can't have muscles and be a fashion cover model? You've shattered my dreams."

"Do not make fun of me."

"Wouldn't dream of it."

"Can we just forget I said anything? I'm sleepy."

"Liar."

She punched her pillow and wiggled down farther under the covers, trying to avoid his gaze. "Good night."

"You have beautiful eyes. They sparkle when you laugh, darken when you're angry…or excited."

Her gaze shot to his and she swallowed nervously. "You…you think my eyes are beautiful?"

"Yeah. Oh, yeah. I love your mouth, too. Those sexy, pouty lips can drive a man wild with fantasies." He ran his thumb across her lower lip, making her shiver. She craved his touch, wanted to feel his hand running down her body, cupping her breasts.

"Your skin is incredibly soft," he whispered, trailing his fingers down her neck to her collarbone, raising goose bumps wherever he touched.

She shifted her legs restlessly beneath the covers. He was setting her on fire, making her ache for his touch. Tugging the covers down to her waist, he slid his hand up under her T-shirt, gently stroking, burning a trail up toward her breasts. She sucked in a deep breath in anticipation but he changed direction.

She grabbed his hand, belatedly remembering she wasn't wearing any underwear.

His gaze met hers as he lifted himself off the covers and flipped them out of the way to the end of the bed.

She quickly smoothed the shirt down to cover her hips, and flushed as he sat down again, his hip pressed intimately against hers.

He stroked her thigh, gently squeezing. "Did I mention how sexy your legs are?" His fingers worked some kind of wicked magic against her skin. She couldn't suppress a little whimper. His hand jerked on her leg and the pressure of his fingers increased as he continued to stroke her.

"Ever since I first saw you I've imagined your incredible legs wrapped around my hips as I—"

"Ryan," she gasped when his fingers touched a particularly sensitive spot. She fisted her hands against the bed and drew in a ragged breath. "What are you doing?"

"I'm trying to make you realize how exquisite you are. All those men who ignored you when you were an accountant were idiots." He leaned down, bracing his forearms on the bed next to her, and pressed a soft, wet kiss against her lips before pulling back.

"Oh." She watched him in wonder as he slid his warm hands back up her thighs.

"I don't know why some man hasn't snatched you up long before now." His fingers slipped up beneath her T-shirt. "But it's not because of your looks. You probably just intimidate most guys because you're smarter than they are."

She gasped when one of his hands traced the underside of her breast. "I…I don't…intimidate you?"

"I'm the cover model, muscle-man type. I don't intimidate easily." He watched her, his eyes so dark they were almost black as he spanned his fingers out and covered her breast. "I want you," he whispered, his voice husky, the skin across his face drawn and tight as if he were struggling for control.

"I want you, too," she whispered, squeezing her eyes shut and arching her back, pressing herself more fully against his hand. Her skin had never been so sensitive before, so…hot, as if every nerve ending in her body was centered on her breast, the movements of his hand sending jolts of pleasure straight to her toes. All her earlier embarrassment was gone. The only thing that mattered now was getting closer to him, touching him and being touched in return.

His hand stilled and she whimpered in dismay, rubbing herself against him like a cat.

As if he couldn't help himself, his fingers moved again, molding her, shaping her in his hand until she thought she would die from the pleasure. "Look at me," he rasped.

She met his gaze, delighted at the heat she saw there.

He shuddered and pulled his hand out from under her shirt.

She watched in confusion as he sat back. The sudden loss of his touch cut through the haze that had enveloped her. She reached for the covers. "Is something wrong?" she whispered.

"If we do this, it needs to be without any pretext between us. I don't want any misunderstandings," he said. "After I get you to safety, you'll go right back into WitSec, and I'll go back to my job. We'll go our separate ways. One day you'll find a man to share your life with you, a man who will be with you no matter what, a man who can give up everything to be with you. I'm not that man. I'm not willing to give up my family, not for anyone. Do you understand?"

His words fell on her like a jagged knife, cutting her heart into little pieces, but she forced herself to meet his gaze. She didn't want him to know how much he'd just hurt her. After so tenderly making her feel beautiful for the first time in her life, treasured, he was boiling it all down now to just sex.

He wanted her, but he didn't want her in his life. He couldn't make it any more clear than he just had.

Her mind screamed at her to stop this, that she shouldn't give herself to a man who didn't care for her the way she cared for him. Did she love him? She honestly didn't know. It was too soon and she didn't trust these feelings yet, especially since the circumstances were so unusual. How many times had she heard about people thinking they were in love because they had shared some traumatic event?

Yes, she should stop this, but in her heart she knew it was already too late. She couldn't turn back now. From the moment they'd entered the cabin and she'd seen the bed, she'd known what she wanted. She wanted *him*. If, by some miracle, they actually made it out of these mountains alive, she didn't want to wonder for the rest of her life what it could have been like to spend one wonderful, amazing night in Ryan's arms.

And if she couldn't have him for more than one

night, she'd just have to learn to live with it. Somehow. She swallowed the hurt, and her pride. She didn't want to think anymore. All she wanted to do was feel.

She tilted her lips up in what she hoped was a sexy smile. "I understand. I still want you to make love to me."

He jerked back. "I didn't expect you to say that."

"I know."

"Are you absolutely sure? I don't want you to have any regrets."

"I'm sure. I know there's no commitment between us. I know I'm not what you want for the long term—"

"That's not what I meant when I said—"

"It's okay. I understand. Your family comes first. I get that. And I'm sure I'm not the picture you've always held in your mind of your perfect woman, of the woman you'll eventually settle down with. We're both consenting adults. We're both here right now. I know there's no commitment and—"

"Jessica."

"We'll just part ways once they find the mole and—"

"Jessica."

"I'll have a new identity and—"

He covered her mouth with one of his hands, his eyes sparkling with amusement. "Do you always talk this much when you're nervous?"

Since he didn't move his hand from her mouth, she nodded.

He caressed her lower lip with his thumb. Heat swirled through her at that one, tiny touch.

"I don't suppose you're on the pill?" he said.

"Ah, no." She did a quick mental calculation. "But I think it's safe."

"You think?"

She didn't think there was any danger of her getting pregnant, but right now she didn't care. All she wanted was to feel his skin against hers, satisfy the burning curiosity and hunger insider her. Rather than let him think too hard about the risks, she reached for him, pulling him down toward her. She pressed her lips against his and slid her hands across his chest, reveling in the smooth, hard planes beneath her fingertips.

He growled low in his throat and returned her kiss, plunging his hands into her hair and anchoring her as he ravaged her mouth.

Gone was the tender, considerate lover he'd been only moments before. In his place was a man wild with desire. For her.

He pulled back and stripped her shirt off, tossing it to the floor. He worshipped her breasts, leaving her panting by the time he started kissing his way down her belly. He eased himself off her long enough to take off his shorts, then he covered her naked body with his. His weight, pressing her down into the mattress, felt so right, like he was the half she'd been missing all her life.

Her eyes widened at the feel of his erection prodding her belly. She reached down between them and wrapped her fingers around him, delighting in the way he shivered when she touched him. He was hot and thick in her hand, velvet-covered steel, and she couldn't resist giving him a long, slow stroke.

He groaned and grabbed her hand. "Careful. I want to last." He kissed her fiercely as he entered her, slowly at first, giving her time to adjust, then faster and faster. His tongue stroked against hers in time with his thrusts, just like Jessica had fantasized.

She couldn't be still. She had to touch him, stroke him, bring him the same wild pleasure he was giving her. She ran her nails down his back to his powerful hips, squeezing, molding the muscles beneath her fingertips, convinced no other man could be this perfect. No other man could ever be…Ryan.

No one would ever take his place in her heart and soul. She screamed as her body climaxed around him. Two more deep thrusts and he hurtled over the edge into ecstasy with her.

Chapter Fifteen

Ryan hated to wake Jessica, but they'd already spent far too much time in the cabin. After the encounter with the gunman yesterday, he couldn't fool himself any longer thinking he'd be able to keep Jessica safe up in the mountains. There were too many variables, too many fronts to cover. He had to get Jessica out of here—now.

After throwing some clothes on and repacking his gear, Ryan gently shook Jessica awake. She was so groggy, he wasn't even sure she *was* awake when he steered her into the bathroom. When he heard the sound of running water from the other side of the door, he hurried outside and climbed up the nearest tree to have a look around.

No sign of anyone following them, but he wasn't taking any more chances. Yesterday had been far too close.

Back inside the cabin, Jessica's face was flaming red and she wouldn't meet his gaze. He hoped she was just feeling shy after all they'd done together last night. He hoped she wasn't regretting anything. He'd been honest with her.

So why did he feel like such a jerk?

He forced his feelings of guilt aside as they left the cabin, but as they headed into the woods he couldn't stop thinking about last night. He kept telling himself to forget how wonderful she'd felt in his arms, and how he couldn't get enough of her, making love to her twice before falling into an exhausted sleep.

When he'd looked into her eyes this morning, it had taken all of his control not to grab her and make love to her again. The only reason he hadn't was because of the urgent need to get her out of the mountains before anyone else caught up to them.

He gritted his teeth and tried again to concentrate on his mission, his goal of keeping her safe. What he really needed was a cold dip in a creek. The icy water was the only thing he could think of that might take his mind off what he really wanted.

Jessica.

JESSICA HIKED BEHIND Ryan, like she had so many times now, only today everything was different. From the moment they'd made love, everything had changed. For her, at least. If they made it out of these mountains alive, Ryan would go back to being a U.S. Marshal. He'd happily leave her behind, no regrets.

Unlike her.

He hadn't lied to her about his intentions. Family was the most important thing in Ryan's life. Jessica had known that even before his declaration last night. She'd seen his love for his family shining in his eyes when he'd told her stories about them.

They'd only known each other for a short time, certainly not enough time for him to decide he cared enough about her to give up everything that was important to him. She couldn't fault him for that.

For her, though, it was different. She'd already given up everything important in her life. And she didn't have a family she had to sacrifice.

But to love her, Ryan would have to give up more than he could bear.

Ahead of her, Ryan held up a branch so she could pass beneath it. He gave her one of his sexy, easy smiles and took the lead again. She sighed and followed him, shoving away her melancholy thoughts. Instead, she focused on being stealthy, on practicing what he'd taught her about leaving almost no trace when she passed through the forest.

She preferred not to dwell on the reason for such stealth. If she let herself think about everything that had happened in the past few days and about the people who were hunting her, she'd become too emotional and unable to function. Instead, she concentrated on blending into her surroundings and keeping alert for any sounds that might tell her if someone was nearby.

They followed a gradual upward slope all day

until they were high into the mountains. It was much colder now than it had been before.

Ryan dropped back beside her. "We're in for some bad weather. I'd like to make it to the next ridge and find a cave to shelter in before it arrives. If we keep going and don't break for a while, are you okay with that?"

"No problem. I'm fine."

He narrowed his eyes and studied her intently, as if he'd heard something in her voice or seen something in her eyes that concerned him. She forced a smile and tried to erase any signs of stress from her face. If he knew how badly she'd fallen for him, how miserable she was inside right now, he'd pity her.

She didn't want his pity.

He finally turned away and took the lead again.

"Ermgph."

Jessica had whispered something in her sleep but Ryan couldn't make it out. After a lunch of beef jerky and crackers that Ryan had confiscated from the ranger's cabin, Jessica had fallen asleep on the ground with her head pillowed on her arms. Knowing he was the reason for the dark circles under her eyes, he'd let her sleep as long as he could, but they needed to get moving if they were going to make it to the rendezvous point he'd arranged with Stuart when he called him at the cabin.

She mumbled again.

"What did you say, sweetheart?"

"Eugene," she whispered, followed by a gentle snort. "Eddie."

He grinned. Even in her sleep she was still trying to figure out his middle name. He crouched down on his heels and gently swept her hair back from her face. "Wake up, sleeping beauty. We have to get going. We need to get to the top of the next rise so I can look around."

Jessica groaned and sat up. "Meaning you want to see if anyone else is following us?"

His warm fingers entwined with hers and he gave her a reassuring squeeze. "While you were in the shower back at the cabin I made a call to my friend, Stuart. He's going to pick us up. All we have to do is make it to a little two-lane road north of here. He'll be waiting for us."

"I don't suppose that little road is just over the top of the next rise, is it?"

He tenderly kissed her lips. "Sorry. We're in pretty deep. That road is a good, long hike from here."

"Then what are we waiting for? Let's go."

"You sure you're ready?"

"No, but let's go, anyway."

He gave her another quick kiss and hauled her to her feet.

THEY REACHED THE top of the next rise, the rise that did *not* have a little two-lane road waiting on the other side. How far away was the road? No point in asking. She wouldn't want to hear his answer.

Ryan was going slower now, although he was still keeping a grueling pace. But at least it was closer to what she could handle. With his long legs, she had to make two strides to his one.

When they reached the top, he said, "I'll have to climb another tree to scout the area. You're coming with me."

"I'm not climbing another tree. No way. That's where I draw the line. No way, never. Forget it."

Minutes later, she sat on a ridiculously thin branch fifteen feet off the ground. Ryan had cast a spell on her. How else could he have gotten her to climb the tree?

His spell only went so far, though. He'd tried to cajole her into climbing higher, but she absolutely refused, so he'd left her in a part of the tree that was well concealed.

He'd hefted himself up the trunk above her with the grace and stealth of a leopard. She couldn't see him anymore, he'd gone so high. The way the breezes shook the branch she was on, she couldn't imagine how he clung to the top of the tree without falling since he was probably hanging on with only one hand and using his binoculars.

Shivering in the cold wind, she watched the forest around her and listened for any sounds. Thankfully, nothing seemed out of place. No more men with guns were roaming around below, at least not that she could see.

The sun was just starting to set when Ryan appeared on the other side of the tree trunk on a nearby branch. Jessica was so startled she almost pitched out of the tree, but Ryan grabbed her arm and steadied her.

"Sugar. You scared me half to death."

Ryan didn't respond, not even to tease her about saying *sugar* again. He wrapped an arm around her waist and scrambled down out of the tree. He set her on her feet, his expression grim.

"What's going on?" she asked. "You're scaring me."

"There's another gunman out there," he said, not mincing words. "He's coming up fast, and he's not some city-slicker crook bumbling around in the woods. He's stealthy, focused, dangerous. We have to get out of here. Now."

Chapter Sixteen

Ryan didn't stop until they reached a small rocky outcrop. He wished he could find a better place to defend Jessica, but he was out of time. He needed her tucked away safe somewhere while he confronted the man who was just minutes away.

He grabbed her, ignoring her squeak of protest, and lifted her over his head. "Grab that rock right there. Haul yourself up onto the ledge."

She grumbled but pulled herself up, with Ryan helping her by lifting her from below.

"Jessica?"

"What?"

He grinned at the irritation in her voice. "Make sure there aren't any bears up there."

"Ryan!"

"Here comes the backpack." He tossed it up on the ledge and she grabbed it.

"Aren't you coming up?" she asked.

"Later. We have company arriving any minute. Get as far back as you can, out of sight. Don't make any noise. Jessie, the phone is in the back-pack. You'll have to put the battery in it to use it. The GPS locator is in there, too. If I'm not back in thirty minutes, call Stuart. He's the first contact under the favorites button. Tell him the coordinates on the GPS and he'll come get you."

"What do you mean, if you're not back? Aren't you coming up here with me?"

Ryan hated the panic in her voice, but he didn't have time to reassure her. "Just be quiet, and call Stuart if things go bad."

"You're leaving me?"

His face tightened at the fear in her voice. "I don't have a choice."

He reached up and squeezed her hand. Then he turned and jogged back into the trees.

As soon as Ryan was gone, Jessica grabbed the backpack and tossed it back down. She turned around, feet first and lowered herself down off the ledge, and dropped to the ground.

She landed on the backpack and rolled to her feet. She tried to throw the pack on her shoulders like Ryan always did, but it was too heavy. She impatiently dug out most of what was in the pack and tossed it aside, keeping only the essentials they would need to make it to where Stuart was going to meet them.

Irritation flashed through her as she tugged the still-heavy backpack over her shoulder. Ryan shouldn't have left her. *She* understood that he didn't want to worry about her while he tried to locate the man who was after them. But what *he* didn't understand was that she wasn't going to sit around while someone took shots at him. Not this time.

What was it Ryan had told her once, in the hospital?

She was going to help him, whether he wanted her to or not.

RYAN WIPED A trickle of blood from his brow and circled his opponent, looking for an opening. Both of them were bloody and bruised and had been trying to get the best of each other for the better part of the last ten minutes.

He didn't know if the other man had a gun or not. They'd both practically run into each other on the path through the woods. Neither of them had the opportunity to go for their guns.

"Who are you?" Ryan asked as he threw a punch that knocked the other man back a few feet. "Who do you work for?"

The man wiped the smear of blood from his mouth and scowled at Ryan. "I'm the man who's going to kill you." He charged forward, wrapping his arms around Ryan's waist, knocking him down.

Ryan struggled to get his hands beneath the other man's jaw, trying to force him back.

"Get off him!"

Ryan froze at the sound of Jessica's voice. She

was standing a few feet away, holding her knife in the air.

The man above Ryan grinned and jumped off him. Ryan shouted a warning at Jessica, but it was too late. The other man had knocked the knife from her hands and grabbed her around the waist.

Ryan drew himself into a crouch, but he stilled when he came face-to-face with the business end of the gun that he'd suspected the stranger had all along. The stranger held Jessica clasped against him, his thick forearm pressed against her neck, forcing her head up at an awkward angle. His gun pointed straight at Ryan.

"Back up. Now," the man said, his eyes narrowing.

Ryan took a step back. He didn't look at Jessica's face. He knew the fear in her eyes would distract him. He needed to focus, to watch for a weakness, an opening, so he could figure a way out of this mess.

"Keep backing up," the man ordered. He pressed his forearm tighter against Jessica's throat.

"Ease up," Ryan said. He held his hands in a conciliatory gesture and quickly stepped back, putting several more feet of space between them.

The man relaxed his hold just enough to let Jessica draw a deep, gasping breath into her lungs.

Ryan risked a quick glance at her face.

She wasn't terrified.

She was furious.

She was also digging her hand into her jacket pocket. What was she doing?

"What do you want?" Ryan yelled, trying to distract the gunman. At the same time he wished he could shake Jessica and make her drop whatever crazy plan she was hatching.

The stranger aimed his gun straight at Ryan's heart, but his arm jerked up in the air, accompanied by his scream as the shot went wild over Ryan's head and the gun fell from his hand.

For a moment, Ryan didn't move. Jessica must have hidden his large hunting knife in her jacket. She'd somehow managed to grab it and stabbed the man's gun arm. The blade had passed all the way through his forearm and was grotesquely sticking out through the top.

The man's screams turned into violent curses. He backhanded Jessica with his other arm, knocking her to the ground.

Ryan roared and drew his gun, but the other man ducked behind a tree, hugging his injured arm across his chest as he ran into the forest. Ryan dropped to his knees beside Jessica. A quick glance at her told him she was all right. He fired off a few more shots into the trees and lunged to his feet to go after the stranger.

"Ryan, if you leave me again, I'll follow you again."

Jessica's threat had him skidding to a stop.

She jumped up and ran to him. "You're a stubborn, pigheaded man. Haven't you learned yet to quit leaving me behind? Let him go. You're too angry. If you go charging after him now, he'll hear you coming. And what about the shots you fired? Surely anyone else who might be after us heard them. Shouldn't we get out of here before they find us?"

Ryan swallowed hard and tamped down his rage. Jessica was right. Charging into the woods like some bull crashing through the undergrowth would just get him killed, and then Jessica would be left to fend for herself.

Although, judging from the damage she'd just done, maybe she wasn't as defenseless as he'd thought. Still, the thought of everything that could have gone wrong when she drew her knife had him feeling sick inside.

He grabbed her shoulders and gave her a small shake. "What were you thinking? You could have been killed. If he'd moved his arm…if the blade had glanced off—" He shut his eyes and took a deep, shuddering breath. When he opened his eyes again, he was still barely in control.

"Don't. Ever. Do. That. Again." He clasped her to him and covered her mouth with his, desperate to feel her against him and assure himself she was okay. When he began hardening, he reluctantly broke the kiss.

"I will never forget the sight of that man holding a gun with his arm across your throat."

"Don't worry," she gasped, reeling from the kiss. "Neither will I. I'm so sorry that I interfered. I thought you needed my help, and all I did was make it worse."

He pulled her to him, hugging her tightly. "If, God forbid, you're ever being held like that by someone, don't try to stab them. Pick up your legs and drop right out of his arms. He won't expect it, and it will leave the way clear for me to shoot him. You got that? No more stunts like you pulled with that knife." He grasped her arms and held her out in front of him. "We need to go back for the pack. My GPS—"

"Is right over there. I stashed the pack behind a tree."

He smiled at her. "You're an amazing woman, do you know that, Jessica Delaney?"

"What? I'm not Jessica Benedict anymore?" she teased.

"No," he agreed. "You're not.

"Come on," he said, grabbing her hand. "Let's get out of here before anyone catches up, and before that man you knifed decides to come back for round two."

A few minutes later, Ryan and Jessica burst out of the forest onto a narrow, paved road. Jessica heard the roar of an engine a split second before a dark SUV barreled out of the trees on the other side of the road. It screeched to a halt in front of them, rocking on its springs.

Ryan trained his gun on the forest where they'd just emerged, shoving Jessica behind him toward the truck. "Get in."

The back door opened and a man leaned out. He grabbed Jessica by the waist and hauled her inside. Then he leaned across her and pulled the door closed.

"You must be Jessica. I'm Stuart Lanier. Pleased to meet you." He winked and reached for her seat belt.

She stared at him in confusion. "Have we met before? You look so familiar."

He hesitated before snapping the seat belt on her. "If that's a pickup line, don't bother. I'm yours already, beautiful." He winked again, but the smile didn't quite reach his eyes. His face was tight with strain. He hopped back into the front driver's seat, sliding his wiry frame in behind the steering wheel.

Ryan jerked the front passenger door open and jumped in. "Go, go, go!"

JESSICA WOKE TO the sound of muted voices. It was still dark outside as the SUV bumped over a pothole in the little two-lane road they were currently traveling on. Ryan was watching the trees roll past their window, keeping guard as he and Stuart spoke to each other in low voices.

Jessica yawned, and Ryan leaned around the side of the seat to look at her.

"We're almost there," he said.

"Almost where?" Jessica asked, stretching and looking out her window. It was still too dark to see much outside and she didn't see any other cars on the road.

"A cheap motel." His mouth quirked up in a sexy half grin. "It's not the Hyatt, but it's not Motel 6 either," he said, echoing her earlier words.

"Are you making fun of me?" she demanded.

"Wouldn't dream of it."

Jessica leaned forward and cocked her head, trying to get a better look at Stuart. "Have you ever been to New York?"

His brows raised and he gave her a grin. "Are you hitting on me again?"

"Again?" Ryan asked, glancing back and forth between them.

"She thinks she knows me from somewhere," Stuart answered.

"If we've met, it will come to me," Jessica said. "I never forget a face."

"I don't suppose you've ever hired Security Services International? My bodyguard and private investigation firm?"

Jessica shook her head. "Sorry. Never heard of it."

"I'll have to give you a business card later. Maybe we met in Afghanistan," he teased. "Although if you were on our A-team I'm pretty sure I would have noticed."

"What's an A-team?"

Ryan frowned at Stuart and turned to Jessica. "Army Special Forces. The team consists of twelve rangers. Stuart served on my team. He was my engineering sergeant."

"An engineering sergeant?" Jessica asked.

"I blow things up." Stuart gave Jessica a cocky grin, then cleared his throat at Ryan's hard stare.

"So, what's our plan?" Jessica asked. "How do I help?"

"You help by doing nothing," Ryan said. "Stuart's going to stay with you at the motel and keep you safe. I'm going to go shake some trees and see what falls out."

"No."

"No?" Ryan echoed, his tone mirroring his disbelief that someone would actually refuse one of his orders. The man really needed to work on his bossiness.

"It's my fault you're in this mess. I'm going to help."

"No. You're not. The last time you tried to help, you almost got yourself killed."

"I also saved your life."

Ryan leaned forward, his eyes narrowed. "If you hadn't gone storming into the middle of the fight, I wouldn't have needed your help."

Jessica crossed her arms and narrowed her eyes back at him. "Your father might have taught you to be just a little too independent. It's annoying. You need to learn to accept help from other people." She glanced pointedly at Stuart. "Or is it just women you don't want help from?"

"There's nothing wrong with protecting women, and keeping them out of danger," Ryan insisted.

She rolled her eyes.

"Besides, Stuart and I have known each other for decades. We work well as a team, and I know he has my back."

Jessica's eyes widened. "And I don't, I suppose? You still don't trust me. That's why you never want me to help you, isn't it?"

His eyes dipped away and his jaw tightened. "I didn't say that."

"You didn't have to." She crossed her arms and fought the urge to kick the back of his seat.

"Uh, Ryan, maybe you should cut her some slack. She's been through a lot." Stuart aimed an apologetic smile at Jessica in the rearview mirror.

Ryan glared at him.

Stuart grinned.

"Just get us to the motel," Ryan said. "And slow down. We don't need to catch the attention of the local cops."

Stuart eased up on the gas and merged onto the interstate ramp.

"Don't waste time with a motel," Jessica said. "Let's go to a computer store. I need a laptop."

"Why?" Ryan asked.

"I wasn't just an accountant for Richard De-Gaullo. I hacked into a few computer systems along the way. That's how I contacted the FBI in the first place. I hacked into the Justice Department's computer system to leave them messages. I couldn't use email. DeGaullo's security team reviewed all of our emails every day."

Ryan's mouth tightened into a hard line, and Jessica belatedly realized she'd never told him that part of her past. The sudden wariness in his eyes had Jessica feeling uneasy.

"That still doesn't answer the question of why you need a computer now," Ryan said.

"I can hack into the Justice Department's computer system, and from there try to hack inside Wit-Sec. I can find out who has accessed my files, who might have known where I'd been relocated. Maybe one of the names will ring a bell and we'll know who's behind everything."

Ryan gave her a hard look before turning around and staring down the highway. Jessica's stomach dropped. Had her admission about her computer hacking undone all the strides forward she and Ryan had made over the past few days? He was her only true ally right now, the only one she could trust. What would it take for him to trust her in return?

"You really think you can figure out who accessed your WitSec files?" Stuart asked, looking doubtful.

"I know I can."

His brows rose. "You're that good with a computer?"

"I'm that good."

"Huh. Maybe you should work for me. I could use a good computer hacker."

"That's illegal," Ryan replied, not looking at either of them.

Stuart shrugged. "Bad choice of words. I could use someone who's good with a computer." He winked and grinned at Jessica.

She ignored him and watched Ryan. He didn't crack a smile, didn't even look at her.

"Cool," Stuart said. "Problem solved, right, Ryan? I'll leave you two at the motel, get a laptop, and have a car dropped off for you." He glanced at the time on the dashboard. "Drive time, a few hours of sleep, waiting for the stores to open, getting another driver to drop off the other car…I should make it back by eleven tomorrow morning, noon at the latest."

Ryan seemed to consider that for a moment. His hand fisted on the seat beside him. He didn't look at Jessica when he finally spoke. "Do it."

Chapter Seventeen

Ryan was quiet as he held open the motel room door for Jessica. He hadn't said much since her comment about hacking into the database. Although he'd grudgingly agreed to have Stuart get the laptop, he still hadn't said whether he'd go along with Jessica's plan.

The motel room, although small, was clean and looked like it had been renovated within the past few years. A flicker of disappointment flared through Jessica when she noted there were two beds. Now that they didn't need to share their body heat to keep from freezing to death, it made sense they should each have their own bed. But she'd grown used to having Ryan snuggled up behind her at night. The thought of sleeping without him had her feeling lonely already, even though he was standing next to her.

"Something wrong?" he asked.

"No, I think I'll grab a shower."

He followed her to the bathroom. Their eyes met

in the mirror and she raised a brow in question. He set the backpack down on the floor, reminding Jessica that Stuart had brought them new clothes and toiletries. "Thank you," she said.

He turned and left without a word.

She had too much on her mind to enjoy the shower like she had back in the cabin. Was she safe here? Did anyone follow them from the mountains? And the thought that shouldn't have mattered as much as the others, but somehow did—was her relationship with Ryan over?

He'd made it quite clear before they'd first made love that they couldn't have a future together. But she'd give anything to see him look at her with desire again, to feel him hold her close to his heart. She could lie to herself, if only for a little while, and pretend he really cared about her.

Since she didn't have a nightgown, and she didn't want to waste the few clean clothes that she had, she wrapped a towel around her body and stepped out of the bathroom, intending to slide under the covers of the nearest bed.

Ryan was sitting on the bed closest to the door reading a newspaper Stuart had gotten them from the motel lobby. His gaze shot to hers and he slowly lowered the paper. The cold indifference in his eyes was quickly replaced by a smoldering heat as his gaze flickered down her body. In spite of the thick towel, she felt totally exposed, and nervous.

She pulled up the covers and slid between the

cool sheets, discarding the towel on the floor. Burrowing beneath the comforter, she grew increasingly uneasy beneath Ryan's unwavering stare. "There's plenty of hot water left," she said to break the uncomfortable silence.

He tossed the paper on the table beside his bed and crossed to the bathroom, firmly closing the door behind him.

RYAN LET THE warm water cascade over his back as he thought back to another shower, the night of the fire. Then, as now, pictures of Jessica flitted through his mind, warming him far more than the water.

Back then he'd hated that he'd responded to her, because he'd despised her. Now, he couldn't stand that he wanted her because he cared far too much for her. No woman had ever twisted him inside the way she did. After hearing about the struggles she'd been through, he'd half convinced himself that maybe she wasn't all that different from him, after all. She wasn't the bad person he'd assumed she was. She'd gotten mixed up in the mob by accident, not by choice. And she'd done the right thing, even though it had taken her a while to gather the courage.

But then he'd seen the excitement in her eyes when she'd talked about breaking into the Justice Department's database. And she'd convinced him to agree to that plan. What did that say about him?

His reverence for justice, for law and order, had been ingrained in him since birth. If someone like him could be talked into crossing that line, what did that mean? Jessica was blurring the lines between right and wrong, making him question everything he'd ever stood for.

He didn't like that one bit, and he was seriously reconsidering whether or not to let her hack into the government's database.

Ryan slammed the flat of his palm against the tile and turned off the water. The shower had done nothing for his raging desires. In spite of everything, he still wanted Jessica more than he'd ever wanted any other woman.

She was in the next room, a thin wall separating the two of them. And yet, right now, the distance between them seemed more insurmountable than when they'd first met.

Unsure what he would say or do when he saw her, Ryan wrapped a towel around his hips and flipped the light off. He opened the bathroom door and discovered Jessica was already asleep, snoring softly in her bed.

A mixture of relief and disappointment swept through him. He lost track of the time as he stood beside her bed, mentally tracing the soft curve of her cheek, watching the gentle rise and fall of her shoulders as she breathed. When she turned on her side, the sheet slipped down, revealing the upper curves of her breasts.

His hand shook as he gently pulled the sheet back up to cover her. Unable to resist the impulse, he leaned down and pressed a whisper-soft kiss on her lips. He crossed to the door and double-checked the lock. The chair he'd propped under the handle was still in position.

He placed his pistol on the table next to his bed and flipped off the light, determined not to think about the incredibly desirable woman in the other bed.

THE WIND WHIPPED the rain in hard sheets against them as Jessica and Ryan struggled down the courthouse steps. Thunder cracked and lightning lit up the sky, silhouetting the dark van at the curb waiting to take them to safety.

Something about that van bothered Jessica and she tried to warn Ryan, but her words were snatched away by the wind and he didn't hear her warning.

The explosion knocked him on top of her. She tried to scream but his heavy body pushed the air from her lungs. She twisted beneath him, struggling to knock him to the side.

"Jessica, Jessica, wake up. Everything's okay, wake up."

Her eyes flew open and she stared up in confusion at the man bending over her in the dark. He was lying on top of her, his fingers wrapped around her wrists.

"Jessie, it's Ryan. Talk to me."

"Ryan?" She blinked as her eyes adjusted to the dim light. "What are you doing?"

He let out a pent-up breath and rested his forehead against hers. She could feel the tension draining out of him as he loosened his hold on her wrists and propped himself up on his elbows. "You were having a nightmare."

"I was?"

"You don't remember?"

She started to say no, but then a crack of thunder sounded outside the room and she shivered beneath him as the horror of her dream came back to her. "The explosion at the courthouse." She shivered again, swallowing convulsively.

He gently smoothed her hair out of her face, then rolled over on his side next to her, propping his elbow on the pillow. "Do you want to talk about it?"

She shook her head. "No."

"Want to watch TV to take your mind off it?"

She shook her head again. "No. Just…just don't leave me, okay?"

He hesitated, and for a moment she thought he would refuse. But then he leaned down and pressed a soft kiss on her lips. He laid his head on the pillow next to her, his body so close she could feel the heat from him. He picked up her hand and entwined his fingers with hers.

Her pulse sped and it seemed her entire body

centered and focused on the warm feel of his hand holding hers.

The sounds of the storm gradually faded as it moved off into the distance until the only thing she could hear was the sound of Ryan's breathing. But it wasn't the deep, even breathing of someone who was sleeping.

"Ryan," she whispered, "Are you awake?"

He squeezed her fingers. "You can't sleep, either?"

"No. Too keyed up, I guess. Why can't *you* sleep?"

He hesitated. "The storm reminded me of another storm, on my last mission."

"One of your ranger missions?"

"Yeah." She could hear his smile in his words. "A ranger mission." He stroked her arm, his fingers absently caressing her skin, then his fingers stilled. "Pretty much everything that could go wrong went wrong."

"What happened?"

His hand tensed on hers. She thought he was going to leave, but instead he pulled her close and kissed the top of her head. "I can't give you any details. Our missions were classified."

"How about a summary. Leave out the super-secret stuff."

He drew a deep breath and wrapped his arm around her waist. "One of our informants, Aamir, betrayed us. I thought he was my friend. We'd worked together for years. He provided intel on the terrorist activities in the region, and his information was always solid, until that last mission. Four men died in an ambush and I realized we had a traitor among us."

"Go on," she urged, when he didn't say anything for several minutes. She rubbed her fingers on the arm wrapped around her waist, hoping he would trust her enough to continue. This was the first time he'd really opened up to her.

"Stuart and I arranged a trap," he finally said. "Basically, we fed Aamir bad information. Then we waited. Sure enough, there was another ambush. But this time, we were ready with an ambush of our own."

"Your friend...did he—"

"He was mortally wounded in the crossfire. I found him, after everything was over. I tried to stop the bleeding, but there was nothing I could do. He could barely speak, but he kept whispering that he wasn't the traitor."

"You didn't believe him?"

"He was the only person we told about the patrol that day. No one else would have known where we were going to be." He stroked her arm, his fingers feathering out across her skin, making her shiver. He grew bolder, stroking down toward her hip.

"I trusted him," he continued, as his fingers blazed a maddening trail across her skin. "For over two years. And with his dying breath he lied to me. I still can't figure out how he arranged everything by himself. He had to have had help. Stuart and I have both examined the evidence, tried to figure out who was calling the shots. No luck so far, but I'm not giving up. I owe it to the men who died to find out who was responsible. I've got Stuart's company investigating it."

The pain in his voice shot straight to her heart. She turned in his arms and wrapped him in a tight hug.

"I'm so sorry your friend betrayed you," she whispered.

He looked deep into her eyes, and then he crushed her against him, claiming her lips with a raw, ravenous hunger that shocked her. She answered him kiss for kiss, touch for touch. This time when the storm raged, it raged inside Ryan. Jessica soothed his wounded soul the only way she could, by loving him.

"ARE YOU GOING to sleep the whole day away?"

"Go away." Jessica squeezed her eyes shut and swatted at Ryan's hand, which was shaking her shoulder.

She hated morning people. How could he be so chipper after they'd kept each other awake late into the night?

He dropped his hand and Jessica smiled with satisfaction, snuggling beneath the covers and sinking back against her soft pillow.

Ryan sighed loudly, as if he was extremely disappointed. "I guess I'll have to eat all of this food by myself. Ham and cheese omelets, pancakes, bacon, fresh-squeezed orange juice."

The smell of bacon wafted to Jessica and she grudgingly opened one sleepy eye. Ryan sat on the edge of her bed waving a thick slice of bacon under her nose. He waggled his eyebrows at her. She frowned and grabbed the bacon.

"Oh, my gosh," she groaned. "This is so good."

He grinned. "I thought you might enjoy something besides granola bars and rabbit for a change."

She looked up at him, and was a little disappointed that he'd shaved the stubble from his face. The scruffy, unshaved look he'd sported back in the mountains made him look less perfect, more like an ordinary mortal instead of the devastatingly handsome man he was right now.

"I can't believe you woke me up this early," she said. "What time is it?"

"You weren't nearly this grumpy sleeping on a pile of branches in a cold cave."

"I'm tired." She pulled herself into a sitting position. "I didn't get much sleep last night." She flushed, wishing she'd chosen different words.

A slow sexy grin slid across his face, but instead of teasing her, he tucked a blanket around her. He stood and grabbed a tray of food from his bed and set it on Jessica's lap. The plate was piled high with food.

"A real plate? A real fork and knife? I'm over-whelmed."

"You can thank me later." He leered at her and she laughed out loud. She'd missed this lighter side of Ryan and was glad to see him smiling again.

She popped a forkful of eggs in her mouth, barely suppressing another moan at the flavor. "Aren't you going to eat, too?"

"I'd rather watch you. More fun."

"Well, don't. You're making me self-conscious. Eat."

"If you insist." He plopped down beside her and she had to grab the tray to keep it from bouncing off her lap.

He plucked a piece of bacon off her plate and shoved it into his mouth.

"Hey, get your own plate."

"Can't reach it. I left it on the other bed." He looked at her with a forlorn expression on his face and dipped his gaze toward her plate.

She rolled her eyes and speared a forkful of eggs. He opened his mouth and she fed him. He closed his lips around the fork and watched her as she pulled it back. He swallowed, then licked his lips, all the time watching her.

Her next forkful was a little unsteady and he had to dip his mouth down to capture it. Again, his lips pulled at the fork as he let her slowly pull it back.

He swallowed and she sat there, frozen as she

stared at him, watching his tongue dart out to lick salt from his lips. She jumped, startled when his hand closed around hers and guided her fork back to the plate. He helped her spear some more eggs, but this time he guided them to her mouth.

With exquisite care, he brushed his thumb across her lower lip. He slid the fork inside. She closed her lips around it and he pulled the fork out, his gaze heating as he watched her chew.

He put the fork on the tray and picked up a piece of bacon. When she swallowed her mouthful of egg, he slid the tip of the bacon between her lips, teasing her by pulling it back so she had to move forward to take a bite.

A bead of sweat ran down the side of his face as he watched her, even though the room was cool. When he lifted the bacon back toward her mouth, she shook her head.

"No more bacon?" he rasped.

"No."

"Eggs?"

She shook her head. "No."

His gaze dipped to her mouth. "Pancakes?"

"Nuh-uh."

He set the tray on the table beside her bed without taking his eyes off her. "What do you want?"

"You. Only you."

"I was so hoping you'd say that," he said just before his mouth claimed hers.

JESSICA'S EYES OPENED. She gasped at the numbers on the bedside clock. It was already after eleven. Stuart was supposed to be here soon, and she definitely wasn't dressed for company.

She rolled over just in time to see Ryan, without a stitch of clothes on, walking into the bathroom. The man had absolutely no modesty.

Then again, when a man looked like he did, there was no reason to hide. Her belly did a funny little flip as she replayed the scene of him walking across the room in her mind. It was her first glimpse of him totally naked without being in near darkness, and she was still reeling when he came out of the bathroom.

He strode toward her, his muscles rippling beneath his golden skin. When her eyes dipped lower, his body immediately reacted.

Her gaze shot to his face as he reached the bed, one of those disarmingly sexy grins curving his mouth seductively.

"I'd like nothing more than to lie in bed all day with you, Jessie, but we have things to do."

He flipped the covers off her and she squeaked in surprise as he lifted her into his arms.

"What are you doing?" she gasped as she was forced to wrap her arms around his neck, her breasts rubbing against the wiry hair of his chest.

"I love it when you blush," he teased. "Everything turns pink."

She groaned and hid her face against his neck.

He let out a deep throaty laugh and carried her into the bathroom, setting her down and planting a quick kiss on her lips. "You have five minutes of privacy. Then I'm coming in to get a shower."

"Five minutes? I can't shower that quickly. It takes me five minutes just to wash and condition my hair."

He looked down at himself, drawing her attention to his growing erection. "The five minutes was for anything else you might want privacy for. I don't expect you to shower alone."

He pulled the door shut.

Her mouth dropped open. He planned on showering with her? In the past day she'd done more things with him than she'd done with any man in her entire life. She'd certainly never showered with a man before. She glanced at the small tub that was barely big enough for one adult to stand in and considered the physics of it.

"Four minutes," he called out from the bedroom.

Her eyes widened. She hurried through her morning routine, ran a brush through her hair and squeezed some toothpaste onto her toothbrush. She'd just started brushing her teeth when he popped his head around the door.

"Time's up."

Her eyes widened as he stepped inside the bathroom. "I'm not ready yet," she tried to say around a mouthful of toothpaste.

"Sorry, beautiful. I can't understand what you're

saying. Your mouth is full of toothpaste." He reached past her and turned on the shower, adjusting the temperature.

She hurriedly rinsed her mouth, just barely finishing before he picked her up and stepped into the tub.

"Ryan, stop it. There isn't enough room in here for both of us."

He pulled her against him, his erection prodding her belly, leaving her no doubts whatsoever of his intentions. His eyelids went to half-mast as he reached down and ran his hands down the curve of her bottom. "Sure there is. Let me show you."

He proceeded to do just that.

Chapter Eighteen

Ryan shut his cell phone off, took out the battery and shoved them both into his pocket.

"Stuart's still not answering?" Jessica asked.

"Something must have happened."

"Maybe he's on his way."

Ryan glanced at the clock beside the bed. "He should have been here by now." He reached down and grabbed the ever-present backpack and put it on. "We're leaving. We've already stayed here too long as it is. Let's go to another motel."

She stepped outside. "What do we do about a car?"

"I've got plenty of cash. We'll get the motel office to call a taxi so we don't leave an electronic trail. After that, I'll figure something out."

THEY TOOK THE taxi north on Interstate eighty-one. They'd only driven a few miles when Ryan directed the driver to take the next exit and pull into a rental car company's parking lot.

Jessica waited in the back of the cab. She was starting to wonder if something had happened to Ryan when a black BMW with dark tinted windows pulled up beside the taxi and Ryan stepped out. He paid the cab, and as the taxi was driving away, he held the BMW's passenger door open for Jessica.

"Actually, I'd rather drive." She ran her fingers lovingly across the roof of the sexy car.

"It's a stick. You can't drive a stick."

Jessica sighed and got in. She was surprised he'd remembered her telling him about that.

He sped out of the parking lot, down the service road.

"How did you rent the car without leaving an electronic trail?"

His jaw tightened. "I bribed the clerk."

She raised a brow. "Was the clerk a woman?"

"As a matter of fact, yes. Why?"

"I see. You flirted with her. Did you give her your number?"

He rolled his eyes and glanced in the side mirror before accelerating up the ramp back onto the interstate.

Jessica had to admit, Ryan really knew how to drive a manual transmission. He shifted smoothly and the car's engine fairly purred as it raced forward.

When they passed a shopping mall and Ryan didn't pull off the interstate, Jessica began to feel uneasy. "Aren't we going to stop for a computer?"

His knuckles tightened on the steering wheel. "I'm not sure the computer's the right way to go."

What was that supposed to mean? Jessica knew she could hack in without being detected. Frustration simmered inside her. She was so tired—tired of running, tired of being afraid, tired of being judged.

Tired of Ryan making decisions without her.

"Is there anything else you planned that I should know about?" She tapped her hands on her jeans.

He glanced at her hand and frowned. "Not really."

She crossed her arms over her chest. "Is that a yes or a no?"

He switched lanes to get around a slow-moving truck. "Is something wrong?"

"Did it occur to you that I might want some input into decisions affecting my future? We agreed I'd hack into the Justice Department."

"That's more of a backup plan."

"I see." She tapped her fingers again and stared out the window.

"What's wrong?"

"Nothing."

"I know better than that."

"Really? You think you know me that well? Don't flatter yourself. Just because we slept together doesn't mean you know a thing about me. Because you don't."

His eyes flicked to her. "What's going on?" he demanded.

"You don't trust me. That's why you don't want to get the computer."

He swore beneath his breath. "I just don't think using the computer is a good idea."

"Then what's your plan?"

"I don't have one yet, other than to lie low. I'll try to contact Stuart later and see what's going on with him. Maybe he had a lead and he'll be able to give us some vital information."

"Are you sure you can trust Stuart?"

His gaze shot to her. "Excuse me?" His tone was icy.

The force of that cold stare had her heart hammering in her chest and she suddenly felt like she'd just crossed a line she didn't even know was there. "Never mind. I shouldn't have said anything."

"Oh, no. You started this. You can finish it. Why shouldn't I trust Stuart? Before you answer, I should warn you that we grew up together in Colorado. We graduated from the same high school. We joined the army together. Why, exactly, do you think I shouldn't trust him?"

She swallowed hard and clutched the seat. "It's just that, well, without me knowing him, things just look kind of…strange."

"Explain." His voice was short, clipped.

She waved her hands in the air in frustration. "I don't know, it's just…okay, at the motel, you told me you trusted that other man, in Afghanistan."

"Aamir."

"Right, Aamir. You knew him for years and he betrayed you. I'm not an expert, but I always heard that men confess their sins when they're dying. They don't tell more lies, not when the end is near and they're worried about their soul. Don't you think it's odd your friend swore he hadn't betrayed you as he lay dying? You said Stuart is the one who helped you set the trap to catch whoever had ambushed your men. Tell me, who shot the bullet that killed Aamir? Was it Stuart?"

His eyes widened, then his jaw clamped tight.

Jessica was obviously right. Stuart was the one who'd shot Aamir.

"What would Stuart's motive be for wanting to kill you?" Ryan insisted. "For that matter, if he wanted to kill you, why didn't he do it when he picked us up in the mountains? Or when we were at the motel?"

"I don't know why he would want to kill me. As far as not killing me after he picked me up, maybe he didn't want to risk hurting you, or he was afraid that you'd kill him if he tried. Or maybe he just wanted an alibi so he could send someone else, like the men in the mountains who tried to kill us."

Ryan jerked the steering wheel, ignoring the honking horns of passing drivers as he fishtailed onto the exit ramp.

Jessica gripped her seat and the armrest as the tires squealed around a curve. Making him angry probably wasn't the best idea while he was driving seventy miles an hour.

He shifted gears and raced down a little two-lane road. A minute later he slowed the BMW to a saner speed and pulled it under a clump of oak trees.

He cut the engine and stared through the windshield at the gravel road. "Get it all out now. Say everything you want to say about Stuart, and then I don't ever want to talk about this again."

Jessica straightened in her seat and narrowed her eyes at him. There was only so much arrogance and bossiness she could tolerate at one time, and she'd just reached her limit. "You want me to talk? Fine. I'll talk. When Stuart picked us up in the mountains, I was convinced I'd met him before, or at least seen him. The only people I was allowed to associate with when I worked for DeGaullo were other people who worked for him. What does that say about Stuart?"

Ryan's faced turned slightly red, as if he was struggling to control his temper.

Jessica plunged ahead. "Stuart is a demolitions expert. Could he rig a toy car to blow up a van?"

"You, of all people, shouldn't question a decorated military officer."

She jerked back. "Me, of all people? You know about my past, the choices I made, and why I made them. I thought we'd moved beyond all of that. I thought you understood and that you'd started to trust me."

"Stuart's not the mole."

"Forget Stuart. I want to know if you trust me. Do you?"

He didn't look at her. They sat in silence for a long time. Jessica finally turned back toward the window, her throat so tight she could hardly breathe.

Ryan swore next to her and started the engine. He floored the gas, sending grass and dirt flying as he spun out onto the gravel road and headed back toward the interstate.

They didn't speak for the rest of the afternoon. Ryan kept driving. Jessica kept wondering how she could have given her heart to a man who looked at her and only saw her mistakes.

When they stopped for gas, she started to get out of the car but he grabbed her arm.

"Where are you going?"

"Unless you want a puddle on the leather seats, I'm going to the restroom."

He studied the parking lot, which was empty except for them. The ladies' room was on the outside of the small food store, to the right, clearly visible from where they were parked. "Okay. But if you're not back in five minutes, I'm coming in after you."

She got out and slammed the passenger door. Three minutes was all she needed, but she took the full five just to spite him. The second hand slowly ticked around the face of the clock on the wall inside the bathroom. Jessica studied her nails and leaned against the sink. Another minute went by.

The door flew open even though she distinctly remembered locking it. Ryan stood in the opening. When he saw her leaning against the countertop, his mouth tightened into a hard line and his eyes narrowed dangerously.

Even though she didn't believe he would ever hurt her, not physically, at least, she barely suppressed a shiver beneath that menacing stare.

She stiffened her spine and stepped past him with as much dignity as she could muster after having him follow her into the bathroom. Ryan followed close behind, closing her car door with far more force than necessary. He peeled out of the parking lot without a word.

A few minutes later, he pulled into a hotel parking lot. Certainly not five-star, but it was nicer than the motel they'd been in the previous night, and much more modern than the ones the marshals had put her in. It was four stories, with no outside access to the rooms.

He kept her with him as he registered, as if he were afraid to let her out of his sight. Guiding her through the lobby, he blocked her from view and herded her into an elevator.

They emerged onto the top floor and he led them down the hall to a room marked "Honeymoon Suite."

She raised an eyebrow when she saw the plaque.

He shrugged, and inserted the key into the reader.

"It was all they had available. There's some kind of convention going on."

The suite boasted a kitchenette with chocolate-brown granite countertops, a flat-screen television in the plush-appointed sitting room, and an enormous bedroom dominated by a king-size, four-poster bed with a canopy and brown silk drapes hanging from each corner.

She peeked into the bathroom, her eyes widening when she saw the Jacuzzi tub sunken into the floor.

Ryan joined her in the doorway, backpack in hand. "If you want to take a bath now I'll order us something to eat."

She glanced up at him, some of her hurt and anger fading at the prospect of getting clean again. "Is it that obvious how badly I want to get in that tub?"

He grinned and for a moment it seemed like none of the tension of the past day had ever happened.

"Baby, you groaned when you saw the tub."

She returned his smile, only to see his smile fade and that shuttered look cross his face again. Their relationship had altered in the past day. It would probably never be the same again.

Without a word, he placed the backpack on the floor beside the tub, then crossed to the door. He was starting to pull it closed when she called out.

"Ryan?"

He hesitated, his hand on the doorknob.

"Thank you," she said.

"For what?"

For giving her a glimpse of what life and love could have been like, even though she knew she would never love another man after him. At least she'd experienced that emotion once in her lifetime, rather than going through her entire life without knowing.

"For protecting me, taking care of me. I owe you far more than I can ever repay."

Some kind of dark emotion flashed in his eyes. Pain? Anger? She wasn't sure. It was gone so fast she might have imagined it. "Quit thanking me. You don't owe me anything." He closed the door behind him.

Jessica sighed, wondering how something so incredibly right had gone so wrong so quickly. After filling the tub with warm water and bubble bath from one of the tiny bottles on the vanity, she slid into the water, groaning with pleasure as the steam rose around her.

She leaned back and tried to blank out her mind and relax. For a few minutes, she just wanted to forget that people were trying to kill her. She wanted to forget the hurt, angry look in Ryan's eyes when she'd told him her suspicions about Stuart.

When the water began to grow cold, she sighed and turned off the jets. Her moment of luxury was over. She'd just started to rise from the tub when a knock sounded on the door. She slid back into the water and grabbed a towel to hold over herself.

"Come in," she called out.

Ryan opened the door and lounged in the doorway with his arms crossed over his chest. His gaze flicked to her towel, then he looked away. The little lines around the corners of his eyes were more prominent than usual. And when he finally spoke, his voice was flat, without emotion.

"All right," he said. "We do it your way."

Chapter Nineteen

Ryan turned and left the bathroom, closing the door behind him.

Jessica didn't know what had made Ryan change his mind, but from the empty, hollow look in his eyes, she suspected he was beginning to have doubts about Stuart. She hoped her fears were wrong, and that Stuart wasn't the one working with DeGaullo to kill her. Ryan had already suffered a terrible betrayal once, and had a hard time trusting anyone, especially her. If Stuart betrayed him, he'd probably never trust anyone else again.

She yanked a comb through her hair, wincing at the tangles. After throwing on her usual ensemble of uninspired jeans and a T-shirt, she rushed through the bedroom to the hotel suite's living area. She paused in the doorway, thinking at first that the suite was empty. Then she noticed the curtains had been pulled back from the sliding glass doors. Ryan was standing on the balcony, his hands shoved into his pockets as he stared out across the parking lot below.

A laptop computer sat on the end table beside the couch, bearing a sticker with the hotel's name. She left the computer sitting there and padded across the carpet to the open sliding glass doors.

"Don't." Ryan's deep voice stopped her just as she was about to cross the threshold onto the balcony. He turned around and leaned back against the railing. "Stay inside, away from the windows. You shouldn't take any chances."

"Neither should you. If you're with me, you're in danger, too." She crossed her arms and stood in the doorway, challenging him.

His jaw tightened and he stepped inside, firmly pushing her back as he closed the doors and the curtains. Ryan might be reckless with his own life, but he would never be reckless with hers.

"I called room service while you were taking a bath." He went into the tiny kitchenette. "The food arrived a few minutes ago." He turned with a tray of covered dishes and carried it to the coffee table in front of the couch. As he raised the covers, Jessica's mouth began to water at the delicious aroma. When she saw exactly what he'd ordered for them, her eyes began to water, too.

For an entirely different reason.

Ryan had ordered steak, asparagus and French fries. Her favorite meal, right down to the side of barbecue sauce. She'd told him that was her favorite meal once when they were hiking through the mountains. She didn't think he'd even been listening. Obviously, he had.

"You remembered," she whispered.

He shrugged and arranged her plate in front of her on the table before sitting back on the couch with his own plate of steak and a baked potato. He grabbed the remote control and flipped the TV to a twenty-four-hour news station.

Jessica ate in silence, casting occasional glances at him. He only pretended interest in the broadcast, because every time she looked at him, he frowned. Then the news reporter gave an update on the story about the courthouse bombing, explaining that unnamed sources had linked the bombing to a house fire in Tennessee earlier in the week. Based on the newspaper found on the lawn, with DeGaullo's picture on the front page, speculation was that Jessica Delaney was the target.

Based on police activity in the area and the teams of trackers in the Smoky Mountains National Park, the reporter theorized that DeGaullo was after Jessica Delaney, and that she might have fled into the mountains with her U.S. Marshal protector. Rumors were the marshal used to be an army ranger.

Ryan cursed and turned off the TV. "So much for government secrecy."

The steak began to sit like a cold hard knot in Jessica's belly. She set her plate back on the tray and pitched the napkin onto the table. "How do reporters get this stuff?"

"I have no idea." He looked over at her. "You didn't eat much."

Jessica glanced at his half-full plate. "Neither did you."

He shrugged and picked up the complimentary newspaper the desk clerk had given them.

Jessica let out a frustrated breath and reached for the computer. She crossed her legs under her on the couch and powered up the laptop. Hacking into the FBI database was just as easy as the first time, even though they'd installed additional safeguards since she'd first contacted them this way.

They really needed better programmers.

"I'm in." Her fingers flew across the keyboard as she circumvented the normal screens and hacked her way into a backdoor. A few minutes later, she'd linked into the server that housed the WitSec files.

An hour later she was still hacking her way through fire walls and encryption schemas, searching for any files that had her name in them.

Ryan set their tray outside in the hallway so room service could retrieve it. He paced back and forth across the suite, occasionally peeking through the curtains to the parking lot as if searching for any threats.

Another hour in, he stopped in front of her, his frustration evident on his taut face. "How much longer?"

"Hard to say. WitSec's security is a lot better than the FBI's security. Depends on how many more layers I have to hack through to get to anything useful."

"Minutes? Hours? Days?"

Minutes, probably. But Jessica didn't want to tell Ryan that, because he'd be hovering over her shoulder the whole time. "Another hour or so."

Ryan tapped his thigh in agitation. "I'm going to grab a shower." He crossed into the bedroom to the bathroom beyond, leaving both doors open. Jessica assumed he wanted to make sure he could hear her if she needed him, but she didn't want the distraction of hearing the water running and knowing he was naked just a few feet away.

Thinking back to the shower they'd shared together had her hands shaking and her mouth watering again. She set the laptop aside and quietly eased the bedroom door shut. Then she went to work on the set of files she'd found that she suspected were the ones she was looking for.

Sure enough, once she broke through the last layer of security she had exactly what she needed. She compiled a list of all the users who'd accessed her files, a surprisingly large list. But most of the accesses were *after* she and Ryan had fled into the mountains, so she eliminated those names. The person who'd set her up would have gotten the information long before the fire that had burned her house to the ground.

Cross-referencing the list of names against the employment database allowed her to remove a few more names. She was banking on her theory that the mole wasn't one of the employees, because Ryan's boss should have had time to investigate all of them thoroughly by now—unless Ryan's boss was the mole. But she'd already eliminated him as a suspect when she'd cross-checked some of the other files.

What she was left with were four names. She didn't recognize any of them. She saved the names to a file on the computer's hard drive and carefully backed out of the Federal database, careful to wipe out any traces that she'd ever been there.

Starting with the first name, she surfed the net to get his bio and current address. This part didn't require anything illegal whatsoever. It was pathetically easy to get the most intimate details about people online. Social networks were the fastest, easiest path to the information she needed. Again she was amazed at what people put out there for anyone to see, never realizing how vulnerable that kind of information made them.

The bedroom door opened. Ryan crossed to the couch and plopped down beside her. His dark hair was damp, slightly curling at the ends. He'd shaved and he was wearing a tight, dark blue shirt tucked into his jeans. Jessica swallowed hard and forced herself to look back at her laptop.

"Find anything yet?" Ryan scooted up next to her to look at the screen.

"Four people accessed my files in WitSec that I couldn't find on the employee database." She punched up the Word document she'd created that contained the information she'd gathered. "I put together short bios and last known addresses on each of them." She paged through slowly so Ryan could see the information. "I couldn't find much about these first three, no more than you can on the average person, anyway. Nothing jumped out at me about any of them."

Ryan read the screen. "Yeah, nothing jumps out at me, either. Who's the fourth person?"

She paged down. "His name is Dominic Ward. He's the—"

"Director of the CIA."

"You know him?"

Ryan's mouth tightened into a hard line. "I know *of* him, but I've never met him. He worked with my C.O. to give us intel for special-ops missions."

"C.O.?"

"Commanding Officer, my boss in the army."

Jessica frowned and studied the picture of Ward, a black and white photo she'd pulled from a newspaper search. "Why would the director of the CIA have access to the Witness Protection database?"

"He wouldn't, not for legitimate reasons, anyway. Search on another name—Alan Rivers."

"Who?"

"Alan Rivers. Alex said he's some higher-up who passed down orders about your case."

Jessica frowned and entered the name into a search engine. Her screen immediately filled with hundreds of hits. "Oh, my gosh. He's the deputy director." Her hands started to shake. "Why is the CIA trying to kill me?"

"Come on. We're leaving." He jumped up from the couch and headed into the bedroom.

Jessica shut the laptop and hurried after him. He already had their backpack sitting on the bed and he was throwing their belongings into it.

"Where are we going?" She stepped into the bathroom to pack their toiletries.

"D.C., FBI headquarters. That's where all the hot-shots are that are looking into the WitSec leak, including my boss. This is way above my pay grade. We're going to show the FBI what you've found."

Jessica's stomach sank. She left their bag of toiletries on the counter and faced Ryan at the foot of the bed. "Show them what I found? Are you crazy? They'll know you let me hack into their database. You could lose your job, or worse. They might arrest you. We can't tell them anything."

He put his hands on her waist and lifted her out of his way.

Jessica sputtered in frustration and followed him into the bathroom. "You can't just walk up to the FBI and say, 'Hey, I hacked into your system and found something interesting.'"

He threw his razor into the bag and zipped it closed. "We don't have a choice."

He brushed past her and put the bag into the

backpack. He tossed it over his shoulder and went into the main room.

Jessica followed, clenching her fists. "Stop for a minute. We need to discuss this. There has to be another way to let the Feds know about this without jeopardizing your career."

"Like what?"

"Not telling the Feds we hacked into their database, for one thing," she snapped.

"Then how do I tell them the director, and deputy director, of the CIA might be involved? We have no proof."

She threw her hands up. "I don't know. You're the covert operations guy. Can't you think of some way to steer them without telling them everything?"

"That's your plan? Lie to the FBI to save my butt? Nope, sorry. I'm not built that way. I don't choose the easy way out to avoid facing the consequences of my own actions."

She stiffened. "Is that what you think about me? That I lie to save myself? That I don't take responsibility for what I've done?"

He shrugged. "If the shoe fits."

She gasped and jerked back. "Well, I guess that says it all, doesn't it? You've never made it a secret how you feel about me."

He swore. "I didn't mean—"

She waved her hand in the air. "Save it. What we need to decide right now is what we're going to do.

Some incredibly powerful people, way more powerful than Richard DeGaullo, are trying to kill me."

"What we are going to do is go to the FBI."

"I don't agree."

He leaned forward, towering over her. "I didn't ask your opinion."

She stomped her foot, enjoying the comical look of surprise on Ryan's face when he straightened.

"I'm sick of you ordering me around," she said. "This is my life we're talking about, not to mention your career, and your life, too. I know your family wouldn't want you to throw your career away, and possibly your freedom if you're arrested, because you were too stubborn to listen to someone else. We have to come up with a better plan."

His nostrils flared and his entire body went rigid. "Leave my family out of this."

"I'm not suggesting we *not* tell the FBI what we found. I'd just like a different way of giving them the information. How do we even know we'll be safe if we walk in there? The CIA could have people everywhere looking for us. How do you know they don't have someone on the inside of the FBI too? How do we know who we can trust?"

Something flickered in his eyes, as if he might be considering what she'd said, as if he might be really listening for a change. "Go on," he said.

Encouraged, she continued. "The only people we can trust right now are standing in this room—

you and me. Until we know for sure who else is involved, we need to handle this on our own."

"And how do you suggest we do that?"

"Actually, I was kind of hoping *you* could come up with a plan for that part."

The corner of his mouth twitched. "You mean, I get to be the boss again? Now that I listened for a change?"

"Ha, ha."

He sobered and stood deep in thought for several minutes. "All right," he said. "Let's go."

"Wait, where are we going?"

He grabbed the backpack and led the way to the door. "Washington, D.C."

Jessica stopped and glared up at him. "I thought you had opened your mind. I thought you were going to consider alternatives?"

He raised a brow. "I did. I am. We aren't going to the FBI."

Chapter Twenty

Ryan flattened himself against the wall of Dominic Ward's spacious, second-floor home office. Getting past Ward's elaborate security system had taken all of Ryan's concentration and nearly an hour of painstaking work. But he'd finally managed to disable the alarm without setting it off. His efforts were about to be rewarded. Footsteps sounded down the hall, coming closer. Ward opened the door and stepped inside. Even though it was well past normal working hours and the sun had set a long time ago, Ward was dressed in a business suit—a suit that probably cost more than Ryan earned in a month. Ward crossed the plush carpet toward his desk, his head down as he studied the papers in his hands.

Ryan clicked the door shut. Ward spun around in surprise. His brows rose when he saw the gun in Ryan's hand.

"Is this a robbery?" His voice sounded more curious than afraid.

"I'm here to talk."

"With a gun?"

"I don't trust you."

"Fair enough." Ward gestured toward his desk. "Do you mind if I sit down?"

"Not there." Ryan waved the gun toward one of two leather chairs facing the desk.

Ward pitched his papers on a side table and sat in the chair facing Ryan. He raised his hand, but froze when Ryan's gun followed the movement.

"I'm just unbuttoning my jacket."

"Slowly," Ryan warned. He sat in the chair across from Ward and rested the pistol on his thigh, pointing it toward the door.

"I'm Dominic Ward, but you probably know that already. Who are you?"

"Ryan Jackson. I'm the marshal protecting Jessica Delaney." He watched for a reaction and wasn't disappointed.

Ward's eyes widened and he leaned slightly forward, a look of interest flashing in his eyes. "The army ranger turned U.S. Marshal, the one who was on the run in Tennessee?"

"I've never heard it put quite that way before. How does the director of the CIA know all that?" he pressed.

"Oh, please, that story is all over the news."

Ryan studied the other man. He didn't look the type to make deals with men like DeGaullo. But then again, what did that type of man look like? Ryan reached into his jacket for the WitSec file—access dates and times that he and Jessica had printed at the business center in their D.C. hotel. He tossed them onto the coffee table.

Ward leaned forward, seemingly unconcerned with the gun Ryan had trained on him. "Is this supposed to mean something to me?"

"Those are the dates and times when you accessed information about Jessica Delaney in the WitSec database." He tapped his finger on the pages. "You and your deputy director are in collusion with Richard DeGaullo. He's got something on you, and in return for his silence, you're helping him try to eliminate the only person who ever had the guts to stand up to him in court."

Ward's eyes widened. The look on his face was one of total amazement. "Please, tell me what proof you think you have. Because, I guarantee, there isn't any."

"I would think the printout is proof enough. If you aren't working with DeGaullo, why would you abuse your access to look at WitSec files?"

Ward picked up the papers and carefully studied them. A look of dawning crossed his face and he turned pale. He started to rise from his seat, but Ryan waved him back down.

Ward gave Ryan a frustrated look. "I need to check my date book. It's over there, on my desk."

"Why do you want it?"

"To defend myself, of course. I assure you I've never even met DeGaullo and I have nothing to do with any of this. I can prove it. My date book, please." He held out his hand as if he expected Ryan to fetch his book for him.

"I don't think so."

"I'll get it." Jessica crawled out from her hiding place beneath the cherrywood desk and grabbed the planner.

Ryan looked at her incredulously. "You were supposed to stay hidden. That was our deal."

"I know. I'm sorry. But I couldn't sit under there any longer. My neck was killing me all twisted up like a pretzel."

"Couldn't you have stayed a pretzel for just a few more minutes? *Sugar*?"

She narrowed her eyes at him. "Are you making fun of me? Again?"

He gritted his teeth. "Wouldn't dream of it."

Ward smiled as Jessica handed the date book to Ryan.

"Can I presume you are the infamous Jessica Delaney?" he asked.

"Infamous. I kind of like that. I—" She squeaked as Ryan shoved her behind his chair and tossed the date book onto the table.

"May I?" Ward paused with his hand over the book. At Ryan's curt nod, he picked it up and thumbed through the pages. He turned the book around and pointed to one of the entries.

"This is when my chemotherapy treatments began. Each of these red lines marks the days when

I began a new course of treatment. I was quite ill for several days after each one. As the Director of the CIA, I have a few perks. One of which is the use of a full-time nurse when I'm sick. My nurse will swear that I never went near my computer while I was going through chemo."

Jessica tugged on Ryan's shirt but he shook her off. He grabbed the date book and checked the entries against the dates on the computer printout. The entries corroborated what Dominic Ward had just said.

"How do you explain the computer log?"

"There's only one other person who could have used my access that way."

Jessica leaned down next to Ryan's ear. "Ryan, you need to see something."

"Just a minute," he told her, staring at Ward. "Who takes care of the day-to-day operations when you're out sick?"

Out of the corner of his eye, Ryan saw that Jessica had crossed the room to a bookshelf. He tried to keep track of what she was doing while keeping a close watch on Ward.

Ward nodded. "Now you're catching up. That's where my deputy director comes into play. I believe you mentioned him earlier. Alan Rivers has been running most everything while I've been out. I've only recently started working from my home while I regain my strength. He had his own log-in ID, so he must have used mine to protect himself if anything like this ever came out." He pursed his lips, his eyes flashing with anger.

Ryan studied him more closely, only now noting the pallor of his skin that suggested a recent illness. His hair was shaved close to his head, like it might be if he'd been undergoing chemotherapy treatments.

Jessica crossed back to Ryan and held a picture frame in the air between him and Ward. Ryan frowned, then stilled as he realized the significance of what he was seeing.

"Show him," he told her.

Jessica turned the picture around to face Ward.

"Who are the men in that photograph?" Ryan asked.

Ward raised an eyebrow. "That's me, of course, on the left. Alan Rivers, the deputy director, is standing next to me."

"That man, Rivers, is the same man who attacked Jessica up in the mountains. She stabbed him with a knife for his efforts."

"Well," Ward said. "I believe you have what you came for, then. Rivers is the one who colluded with DeGaullo. Not me."

"One of the other men in that photograph was in the mountains, too." Ryan pointed to a man on the right side of the group photograph, the rifleman he'd killed. "Do you remember his name?"

Ward squinted at the picture. "No, I can't say that I do. I'm afraid I don't recall any of the other men's names in that picture, but they all work for the same company, a security company that helps us with logistics overseas."

A feeling of foreboding crept through Ryan. He held his breath, praying the terrible suspicion in his mind was wrong. "What's the name of the company?"

"Security Services International."

Stuart's company.

Jessica sucked in a sharp breath.

Ryan shoved his gun into his waistband and clenched his hands together. Everything he'd believed when he began the confrontation with Dominic Ward had just turned upside down. His gut clenched and all he could think about was betrayal; that a man who'd been his friend from the time he was in grade school had betrayed not only him, but his fellow soldiers.

And the marshals.

And Jessica.

He looked up at her. "You were right about Stuart all along."

"I'm so sorry," she whispered.

He grabbed her hand and held on tight. "You said the company helps you with overseas logistics?"

"Yes," Ward said. "Pretty much anywhere top-secret missions are involved that require covert support. It's a fairly new company. Rivers recommended them. He said he met the owner while in Afghanistan a few months ago, before the company was launched, and knew he could do some great work for us."

Jessica set the picture frame down on the table. "I don't understand where I fit in here. What does DeGaullo have to do with Stuart's company? Why is Rivers trying to kill me?"

Ryan sighed heavily and stood. He put his hands on her shoulders. "You're not the target. You never were. I am."

Her eyes widened. "What?"

"When the government's investigation into my team's deaths on our last mission stalled, I hired Stuart's company to look into it. He knew I wouldn't let this go. He must have been behind the ambushes all along. He must have met Rivers when we were in Afghanistan and cooked up a scheme to skim money off defense contracts. Someone on my team saw him, or somehow figured out what he was planning."

He squeezed her shoulders. "The only tie-in to DeGaullo, that I see, is you. Which means, Stuart and Rivers used you as a pawn. They wanted to kill me to keep me from exposing them. So they framed DeGaullo, making it look like he was trying to kill you, so my death would just look like collateral damage and no one would make the connection back to Stuart or Rivers."

She blinked several times, as if she was trying to soak everything in. "Then the explosion at the courthouse—"

"Was probably meant for me. Rivers had my boss assign me to your case at the last minute. But he didn't know how WitSec worked. He didn't realize your security detail was all set, and that my boss was just having me bring over the final paperwork. He probably assumed I'd be in that van with you. I'm so sorry, Jessica. I blamed you for the deaths of those marshals, when it was my fault all along. I should have trusted you. I didn't realize…"

She pressed her fingers against his lips. "None of this is your fault. Stuart and Rivers are the ones to blame."

"I'm not sure I follow," Ward said, looking back and forth between them.

Ryan's mouth flattened. "Stuart Lanier is the one who owns that company you mentioned. His men are the ones in that picture who came after Jessica and me in the mountains. Based on what you said, I think he and Rivers are skimming money on defense contracts. It makes more sense than them working with DeGaullo. They can make a lot more money off the government than an organized crime boss."

Ward nodded. "I'll do whatever I can to help."

Ryan put his arm around Jessica's shoulders. "When you asked Stuart where you two might have met, I started to suspect he was somehow involved. But I didn't want to believe it. After you mentioned your own suspicions, it made me angry, mainly because I was thinking the same thing, and I didn't want to believe that someone I'd trusted for years could do something like this."

She put her arm around his waist and leaned against him. "I remember where I saw him now, and why he looked so familiar. He was at the courthouse. He passed right by us when the marshals were leading me down the hallway. It struck me as odd, because they usually didn't let anyone get that close to me."

Ryan hugged her harder against his side. "All of them knew Stuart. They knew he was a friend of mine."

Ward crossed to his desk. "I'll call my office and have them contact the Justice Department. Based on your eyewitness accounts, I imagine there's enough justification to issue a warrant for Rivers and this Stuart fellow, to bring them in for questioning."

He picked up the phone and frowned. He punched the buttons several times. Then he glanced sharply at Ryan. "The phone is dead."

The lights went out, plunging the room into darkness.

Chapter Twenty-One

Jessica clutched Ryan's hand. Had Stuart followed them from the hotel? Was Rivers with him, eager for revenge because she'd stabbed him? She looked up at Ryan for reassurance. But even though the room was dark, the moonlight filtering in through the windows was enough for her to see the grim look on his face.

He handed her his cell phone and battery. "Call 9-1-1. Tell them there's an intruder, and a federal officer needs assistance. Make sure they know what I'm wearing so they don't shoot *me* instead of a bad guy."

"Wait." Jessica grabbed his arm as he started to turn away. "Don't go, please. Wait for the police."

His face softened and he put his hands on her shoulders. "I'm not abandoning you. I need to see what we're up against and tilt the odds in our favor."

Her face flushed and she knocked his hands off her shoulders. "I'm not worried about *me*. I'm worried about *you*. Can't you wait for backup?"

The sound of breaking glass drifted up from downstairs.

Ryan stiffened. "Whoever's down there is probably armed, and he knows we're up here. We can't wait for the police." He looked over at Ward who was silently watching them. "Do you have any weapons?"

"No." He cursed and shook his head. "I don't keep weapons at home. I don't want to risk my grandkids getting hold of them when they come over." He gave Ryan a sour look. "Until you came along, I thought my security system would keep me safe."

Jessica cupped Ryan's face to make him look at her. "What if Stuart is down there? He has special-ops training, just like you. What if he set some kind of trap?"

He raised a brow, looking as arrogant as when she'd first met him at the courthouse.

"I trained Stuart. He's good, but I'm better." He glanced around the room, his gaze settling on the desk by the window. "Help me move the desk to the other side of the room," he told Ward. "You can use it to block the door after I leave."

Jessica pursed her lips and snapped the battery into the phone. She punched the buttons far harder than necessary. While she tried to explain to the operator what was happening, the men heaved and shoved the heavy desk across the thick carpet to the door. When they were finished, Ryan drew his gun, and slipped into the hallway without a backward glance.

Why was he being so stubborn? Why couldn't he wait for help? Jessica gritted her teeth.

Ward flipped the lock and scooted the desk until it was snugged up against the door.

Another crash sounded downstairs, followed by a terrifyingly familiar dull roar. The blood rushed from Jessica's face as the faint smell of gasoline and smoke leaked into the room. Her gaze shot to Ward and her hand tightened around the phone.

"The house is on fire," she told the 9-1-1 operator, before tossing the phone on the desk. "Help me get the door open. Hurry."

Together she and Ward shoved the heavy desk back enough so they could fit through the opening.

"Hold it." Ward grabbed Jessica's arm when she tried to squeeze past him. "I should go first."

She didn't waste time arguing. She had to get to Ryan. Every second counted.

Please. Let him be okay.

As soon as Ward cleared the doorway, Jessica whipped around him and bolted down the hallway. Panic squeezed her chest when she saw the orange glow ahead, casting flickering shadows on the two-story wall from the foyer below.

At the top of the stairs, she stumbled back in dismay. Fire had already consumed the bottom half of the stairs. Greedy flames licked at the railing, steadily creeping toward the second floor.

"Jessie!" Ryan appeared in the smoke below, standing in the middle of the marble floor, the only part of the foyer that wasn't on fire.

"Up here!" she called out.

"Where's Ward?"

"Over here." He stumbled forward, aiming a baleful glance at Jessica.

"Is there another staircase?" Ryan ducked and jumped to the side when a chunk of burning wall crashed down beside him.

"This is the only way down." Ward coughed violently, looking pale and fragile.

Flames whooshed into the air as another section of staircase caught on fire.

Ryan ducked away. "Tie some curtains together, bedsheets, whatever you have to do. Climb out a window and get out of here. Hurry, the entire front of the house is going up."

"No." Jessica frantically shook her head. "I'm not leaving without you."

The deafening crack of a gunshot echoed in the foyer. Ryan dove to the floor and rolled to the other side of the staircase. Ward shoved Jessica down on the floor.

"Ryan!" Jessica shook Ward off her and squinted through the railings into the smoke below, but she didn't see him anywhere. "Ryan!"

Ward pulled her to her feet and tugged her away from the railing. "There's a dormer in the master bedroom. We can get out on the roof, lower ourselves to the garage. Come on."

They both leaped back as flames reached the top of the stairs, spilling onto an area rug where the wooden floor met the staircase. The fire quickly spread to a nearby decorative table. A vase on top of the table exploded, raining shards of glass down onto the floor.

Jessica coughed and stumbled back from the heat. How could Ryan survive this? Was he shot? Was he lying on the floor, already dead? Hot tears tracked down her cheeks.

"Miss Delaney, please, we have to go." Ward tugged her away from the flames.

"There has to be another way. Maybe we can lower ourselves over the railing—"

"If we stay much longer, we'll both die."

"Go on without me." She tried to run back toward the stairs, but he wouldn't let go.

"I'm not leaving you, Miss Delaney."

Her gaze shot to his and she read the truth of what he'd said in his eyes.

The tears fell harder now and she had to blink to clear her vision. She glanced back toward the banister again, but it was already engulfed in flames. Ryan had proven time and time again how capable he was. No matter how bad things looked, he usually came out on top. But this time, she was terrified his winning streak might have finally run out.

"All right," she said, her voice breaking. "Let's go."

RYAN CROUCHED DOWN beneath the curtain of smoke. He held his gun out in front of him, making wide sweeping arcs as he searched for whoever was taking potshots at him. From what he could tell, there was only one intruder, but he'd started fires all over the front of the house. The only reason Ryan wasn't roasting alive was because of the massive expanses of marble floor, acting as a fire barrier.

He clenched his jaw as he looked back at what had once been the stairs. Jessica had proven that she was a survivor, a fighter. She'd make it out of the house. She'd be okay.

He had to believe that.

A shoe squeaked off to his right. He dove to the ground and squeezed off two quick shots.

WHEN THEY'D REACHED the single-story roof of the garage, Ward slipped and fell, dragging Jessica with him. He'd landed on the shrubs below, and Jessica had landed on top of him. She was scratched up and bruised, but he was in far worse shape.

She helped him limp a safe distance away because he couldn't put any weight on his right ankle. From the way Ward seemed pained every time he drew a breath, Jessica suspected he had at least one broken rib. She eased him back against a tree, and helped him slide down onto the grass.

Jessica glanced back at the house, and started to get up, but Ward wouldn't let go of her arm.

"Uh-uh. You're not sneaking past me this time.

You're not going back to that inferno. It's too dangerous."

Several loud bangs sounded from the house. Renewed hope surged through Jessica. "Those were gunshots. That means Ryan's still alive, and he's fighting for his life. I have to help him." She twisted violently, but Ward held on with surprising strength.

"He wouldn't want you to help him."

Ward was right. Ryan was stubborn about her helping him, and in truth she'd been more of a hindrance than a help in the past, but she couldn't sit on the lawn and just hope that he was okay.

"Let me go, or I'm going to have to hurt you," she said.

He smiled. "Oh, I don't think you would—"

Jessica punched him in the groin.

Ward gasped and hunched over, clutching himself.

"I'm so sorry," Jessica yelled back, as she tore off across the sweeping lawn toward the house. The ruined front doors sagged open. Beyond them, flames seemed to cover every square inch of available space, belching out thick, black smoke. Ryan was in there somewhere. She had to get him out.

She remembered what he'd said, about the *front* of the house going up. Maybe the fire hadn't reached the back yet. Clinging to that hope, she sprinted across the grass to the side yard and around the corner to the back of the house. Smoke seeped from around the windows and doors, but she didn't see any flames.

She yanked at the doors, but they were locked. Grabbing a clay pot from the patio, she heaved it toward one of the sliding glass doors. The pot shattered, pouring black dirt and winter flowers onto the patio, but the door remained intact.

Every curse word she'd ever said as a teenager came pouring out of her mouth. She frantically looked around for something else to throw. Nothing but more pots, too large and heavy for her to pick up.

There had to be a way to get inside! She raced along the back of the house to the other side, nearly weeping with relief when she found a French door with a latticework of delicate-looking glass panes. As expected, the door was locked, but several well-aimed kicks to one of the glass panes shattered it into tiny pieces that sprinkled down onto the floor inside.

She reached her arm through the hole and unlocked the door. Yes! She was inside, racing through the kitchen and out into the main hallway. Superheated air blasted at her. Burning embers rained down from above.

Her shoes slipped across the soot-covered floor. She raised her hands to shield her face from the heat. Struggling to keep her balance, she rushed toward the back of the house, away from the flames.

The marble floor acted as a fire break here. A

smoky haze filled the air, making her cough and choke. She pulled the neck of her shirt up and covered her mouth and nose to filter out the smoke.

Raised voices sounded off to her right. She followed them into what must have been the family room, dotted with couches and chairs. Stuart and Ryan faced off in the middle of the room, fifteen feet apart. Jessica ducked down behind one of the couches, and peeked around it. Stuart was pointing a gun at Ryan's chest.

Ryan was unarmed.

Where was his gun? There, on the floor, a few feet away from him. Stuart must have surprised him and forced him to drop his weapon. Damn Ryan for being so arrogant and running downstairs when he could have stayed upstairs with her and Ward. If he had, he'd be outside right now. He wouldn't be staring down the barrel of a gun.

Sirens sounded in the distance. Help was finally coming, but would they be too late? Jessica fisted her hands on the floor. There was no way she could reach the gun—not without being seen. Maybe she could distract Stuart and give Ryan a chance to grab his gun. That hadn't worked out so well back in the mountains. But what else could she do? Stuart was about to shoot Ryan. He didn't have a chance unless she did something. She inched back into the cover of smoke.

"Why didn't you just kill me when you picked

me up in the mountains?" Ryan's voice rang out. "Or at the motel?"

"It's cleaner this way. The director has a lot of enemies."

"Oh, right." Ryan sneered. "That's your preferred game. Frame other people for what you did. Tell me it wasn't for money. Please tell me there was another reason, anything."

"I was about to lose my house." Stuart's voice was laced with bitterness and regret. "It was easy money. No one was supposed to get hurt."

"You sabotaged the mission, killed four of our fellow soldiers," Ryan snarled.

"They saw me talking to Rivers. I didn't have a choice."

"What about Aamir? Did he have a choice? Was he in on it with you?"

"He figured everything out. He was going to tell you. I had to stop him."

Ryan swore. "All this time you let me believe he'd betrayed me."

Jessica crept forward. She could see them both again. Just a few more feet.

Stuart's knuckles whitened where he gripped the gun. "I was trying to protect you by giving you someone to blame for what happened. Why couldn't you just believe my story? Why did you have to keep digging? You're the last person I wanted to hurt. You're like a brother to me."

Ryan took a menacing step forward. "You're no

brother of mine." He took another step, as if he didn't care that Stuart was pointing a gun at him. "Did it even matter to you that Jessica Delaney had to die to make your little plan work? When does it end? How many more lives will you sacrifice to satisfy your greed?" He took another step, crouching down as if he was going to launch himself at Stuart, even though he was still at least ten feet away.

"Stop." Stuart's face flushed and he took a step back. "Don't come any closer."

What was Ryan doing? He was deliberately baiting Stuart. Jessica had to do something before it was too late. She inched forward, emerging from the smoke just a few feet to the side and slightly behind Stuart.

Ryan's eyes widened, then they narrowed and every line in his body went rigid. He'd obviously seen her, even though he didn't look directly at her. Jessica could tell he was furious. He would never want her to deliberately put herself in danger.

Tough.

She'd hidden beneath a desk when DeGaullo killed Natalie. She was *not* going to cower again and let Ryan die. She'd rather die herself than live knowing she might have helped him but she did nothing.

Flames raced across the far wall, finally reaching this section of the house. The wallpaper ignited like a torch. In a matter of seconds the entire back wall was consumed. Flames curled around the windows and the glass exploded.

Stuart ducked and raised his arms to protect himself.

Ryan rushed forward.

Stuart cursed and swung his gun around, firing a shot. Ryan slid to a halt on the polished floor and raised his hands in a placating gesture. His jaw tightened when he glanced at the arm of the chair, just inches away, where the bullet had lodged.

"I didn't want to do this." Stuart's voice was rough, barely above a whisper. "Forgive me." He steadied the gun, aiming at the center of Ryan's chest.

Jessica shouted and leaped forward, knocking his gun arm just as he fired. The bullet whined harmlessly into the ceiling above as Jessica fell to the floor at Stuart's feet.

Ryan dove for his gun.

Jessica scrambled to get out of the way, but Stuart grabbed her. He yanked her in front of him as a shield just as Ryan came up with his gun.

Ryan's mouth twisted with disapproval, his dark eyes staring directly at Jessica for the first time. "Stupid woman. Didn't you learn anything from the confrontation with Rivers?"

She stiffened with shock at his contempt-filled words, but when his gaze dipped to the floor, she realized he was trying to give her a signal without alerting Stuart. She gave him a slight nod, letting him know she understood.

Stuart shoved his gun against her temple. "Drop your gun, Ryan." He backed toward the gaping hole where the windows used to be. Flames, hungry for fresh air, licked eagerly at the opening.

Ryan laughed harshly. "Do you honestly think I care what happens to her? She's a criminal, a mafia whore. She disgusts me."

Jessica jerked back against Stuart. Ryan's words cut like a knife. Was he just trying to make Stuart think he didn't care what happened to her? Or did he really mean those awful words? He certainly sounded convincing.

Stuart must have thought the same thing. He turned his gun back toward Ryan.

"Now, Jessica!" Ryan yelled.

She picked up her feet and dropped right out of Stuart's arms.

Ryan fired once, twice, running forward and scooping Jessica up before Stuart's lifeless body crumpled to the ground.

He leaped through the hole where the windows used to be and didn't stop running until he reached the cool grass, far away from the devastation behind them.

He dropped to the ground, coughing violently, before pulling Jessica onto his lap. He cradled her against his chest and rested his cheek against the top of her head. "Did Ward make it out?"

She drew in a shaky breath, still reeling from the words he'd said to Stuart. "I think he cracked a rib, or at least broke his ankle when we fell off the roof, but he's—"

He yanked her back to look at her, his face pale. "You fell off the…" He squeezed his eyes shut and crushed her against his chest again. "Why did you run back into the house? You should have waited outside."

"And let you die? I don't think so."

He pulled her back again and stared down at her. His face was drawn. His whole body was shaking. He looked like he wanted to strangle her.

"Drop your weapon!"

Ryan jerked around at the sound of the voice.

"Drop it now!"

Two policemen stood a few feet away, both of them pointing their guns at Ryan. Back toward the house, a caravan of fire trucks and police cars wound their way up the drive, their red and blue lights flashing.

"Federal officer." Ryan slowly raised his hands, pointing his gun up in the air.

"Toss the gun away," one of the policemen ordered.

Ryan pitched the gun onto the grass.

While one of the policemen trained his gun on Ryan, the other one ran forward, kicked the gun out of the way, and grabbed Jessica, hauling her back several feet.

"Are you okay, ma'am?"

Jessica tugged her arm out of his grasp. "What are you doing? He's a U.S. Marshal."

"Holster your weapons, gentlemen." A man in a dark business suit strode across the grass and stopped beside one of the cops. "I can vouch for Marshal Jackson."

The policemen gave him a curt nod and put their guns away.

The man in the suit reached down and hauled Ryan to his feet. "Hell of a mess, Jackson."

Ryan gave him a rueful grin. "Jessie, this is my boss, Alex Trask."

Alex raised a brow at Ryan's use of the nickname, but he turned and offered his hand. "It's an honor to finally meet you, Miss Delaney."

"An honor?" Jessica echoed, shaking his hand.

"You're the only person I've ever met who had the courage to stand up to DeGaullo." He grinned. "And you're probably the only person in the world who could punch the director of the CIA in the groin without getting hauled off to jail."

Jessica flushed as Ryan's incredulous gaze focused on her.

He shook his head. "I don't even want to know."

Alex motioned toward two other men in business suits who were crossing the grass toward them.

"Miss Delaney, these marshals will take you back into protective custody while I get the scoop on what happened from Marshal Jackson."

"Wait," Ryan said. "Can you give us a minute?"

Alex didn't look like he wanted to, but he nodded. "Okay, but make it quick. I want her back in custody before DeGaullo figures out where she is. And you and I are going to have a thorough discussion about following orders."

He motioned to the marshals and the two policemen who were standing a short distance away. The small group headed back toward the house where dozens of law-enforcement officers were milling around while the firemen worked to get the blaze under control.

The look of regret on Ryan's face was already breaking Jessica's heart before he said a word.

"Now that we know who was behind the Wit-Sec leak, it's safe for you to go back into the program. Alex will arrange a new identity and location. You'll get a fresh start…again."

Jessica twisted her hands together so Ryan wouldn't see how badly they were shaking. "You're leaving? Just like that?"

"You knew it had to end this way."

"Would it make a difference if I told you I love you?"

Ryan winced and looked away.

Jessica blinked against the unwelcome rush of tears at the back of her eyes. "I guess that answers that question."

"I'm sorry, Jessie." He reached for her.

She ducked away, backing up several steps. If he

touched her right now, she didn't think her heart would survive. "Did you mean those things you said to me, back at the house, in front of Stuart?"

His brows wrinkled in confusion. "What are you…" His eyes widened. "No, no, of course not. That was a lie, a complete lie, to get Stuart to turn the gun away from you." He reached for her again.

She sidestepped him and put several more feet between them.

Ryan blew out a frustrated breath. "I care about you, Jessie, very much. I know you aren't the person I thought you were when I read your file. But it doesn't change anything." His mouth tightened into a flat line. "I love my family, very much. I can't give them up and go into WitSec to be with you. My family means everything to me."

And you don't.

The words hung in the air between them just as surely as if Ryan had said them out loud.

"Well, then. I guess that says everything, doesn't it?" Jessica said bitterly.

Ryan's eyes filled with regret. "Jessie—"

A shout echoed across the lawn. Alex was waving to get Ryan's attention.

"Go on," Jessica said. "There's no point in dragging this out any longer." She pasted a smile on her face and held out her hand, pretending she wasn't dying inside. "Thank you for protecting me. I owe you my life."

His eyes flashed with anger and he ignored her hand. "It's a bit late to act all formal now."

She dropped her hand.

He sighed heavily. "Don't thank me for saving your life when we both know you saved my butt back there. I have to say, that was a humbling experience. All my life I've been the one who charges in without waiting for help. I'm the one everyone else looks to. But you nearly died in the fire because I was too stubborn to listen, to wait for backup, or to just get you and Ward out of the house instead of charging downstairs. And even though I didn't want your help, you went into a burning house to help me. Next time, I won't be so stubbornly independent that I can't accept someone's help when I need it."

She gave him a half smile. "Hopefully there won't be a next time, right? You'd better go. Your boss looks like he's getting mad. Don't worry about me. I understand everything, and I'll be fine." *Eventually.*

Ryan glanced at Trask, then back at her. He narrowed his eyes. "What do you mean, you *understand*?"

She frowned. "Family means everything to you. They come first, and they should. When I first went into WitSec, I remember thinking that if I had to give up a family, I couldn't do it. Loving someone that much, to give up everyone else in their life for them…" She shrugged. "I would never expect that. I understand."

He closed his eyes and a pained look crossed his face. When he looked at her again, his eyes were sadder than she'd ever seen them. "I wish it could have been different," he whispered. He stepped forward and pressed a soft kiss on her lips. "You're an amazing, strong woman. You're going to be okay, Jessica Delaney."

He turned away, and literally walked out of her life.

Chapter Twenty-Two

Within days of Alan Rivers being convicted, the Justice Department had given Jessica a new identity and whisked her away to her new home. Another rural cabin, another mountain range in her backyard. If Jessica had been given a choice, she wouldn't have chosen to relocate to Nevada, because she could see the Rocky Mountains out her back door—the same mountain range in Ryan's home state of Colorado. She wasn't sure her heart could survive the constant reminder of the man she'd loved and lost, every time she went outside.

The rural part, however, she could definitely handle. Since moving in over a month ago, she'd grown to appreciate the quiet, the isolation. Alone, she didn't have to face the pressures of answering questions with memorized lies. Alone, she didn't have to face the curious glances, and questioning stares, when a stray memory of Ryan flashed through her mind and unwelcome tears tracked down her cheeks.

She stepped out the front door, clutching her jacket against the frigid temperatures. The promise of snow hung heavy in the air, and the frozen gravel crunched beneath her shoes as she started down the road for her morning walk.

The throaty roar of a motorcycle had her moving to the shoulder of the road just as an achingly familiar black bike crested the ridge and pulled to a halt beside her. The driver, dressed in jeans and a leather jacket, turned off the engine. Even before he took off his helmet, Jessica knew who he was by the way her heart squeezed in her chest.

Ryan Jackson.

Jessica was going to kill Alex Trask.

"Hello, Jessie."

The tenderness in his voice confused her. She didn't want him to hurt her again, but *sugar,* it was so good to see him.

She knew she couldn't trust him with her heart. She'd never survive him walking out of her life again, so she couldn't let him back in to begin with. But she'd also learned something else, about herself, after everything she'd been through. She'd learned that she *did* have value. She *was* worth saving, only this time, she was saving herself.

"What are you doing here?" she asked, purposely making her voice cold, disinterested. "Did Alex send you to check up on me, to make sure I'm not slipping back to my criminal roots?"

He winced. "I suppose I deserved that. Alex

didn't send me. I'm not a marshal anymore. I'm here for a more personal reason."

Her pulse leaped crazily, but she cruelly squelched the hope that burned in her chest. She couldn't afford to hope. "Isn't this against some precious Wit-Sec rule or something?"

"I bribed a clerk." He gave her a lopsided grin that had her heart doing flip-flops. "Actually, you'd be surprised what the Justice Department will allow if you agree to help them cover up a major fiasco to protect their reputation, and their funding." He held out his hand. "Ride with me."

She took a wary step back. "No."

Undaunted, he pulled a helmet out of his other saddlebag. "Ride with me."

Jessica frowned at him. "Why?"

"Because I ran into a burning building to save you?"

She cocked her brow. "Ditto."

"Double ouch. Okay, I didn't want to force your hand, but either you take a short ride with me and let me say what I came to say, or I park my butt outside your bedroom window and sing all night long. You won't sleep a wink. Trust me. I'm a lousy singer."

She huffed and grabbed the helmet, irritated that she wasn't immune to his charm. "You know how much I hate these torture machines."

"I know. Thank you," he said, pressing a quick kiss to her lips before she could duck away.

She felt that fleeting kiss all the way to her toes.

He adjusted the fit of her helmet, and slid his fingers through her newly blond bangs, pushing them out of her eyes. "I liked your natural color better."

"This *is* my natural color. I dyed it brown when I first went into Witness Protection." She slung her leg over the back of the bike and sat down behind him.

"I guess I'll get used to it," he said.

Her heart caught at his words, but he started the engine, and then she was too busy holding on to ask him what he'd meant.

After winding down the mountain, and turning down a long two-lane road she'd never driven down before, he pulled the bike to a stop in front of an enormous, two-story log cabin. Bright, new wood railings and window casings contrasted against the aged wood of the rest of the house. Scraps of logs and fresh lumber riddled the front yard.

"We're here," he said, cutting the engine.

Jessica realized he was waiting for her to dismount. She swung her leg over the bike, and hurried up the steps to the cabin's massive front porch to avoid the hand Ryan had held out for her.

"Let me show you the main hall." Ryan grabbed her wrist and hauled her inside.

She had to jog to keep up with his long strides. He didn't let her go until they were in the main room. The interior was stark, utilitarian, unfinished. What looked to be office chairs lined one side of the room, and rows of long, metal tables lined the other wall.

"This is where the kids will learn computer skills," he said.

"Ryan, why are we—"

"Wait until you see the barracks." He towed her after him again, down the back steps.

"Did you say barracks?" She was breathing hard, trying to keep up with him.

"Yep."

He pulled her inside a much smaller version of the main cabin. The building was long and narrow and only one story. Rows of metal cots were stacked around the room, much like an Army barracks might look, or at least the barracks Jessica had seen in movies.

"What is this place?" she asked.

"It's a camp."

She glanced around in surprise. "Doesn't look very comfortable, or fun."

"It isn't supposed to be fun. This is where the tough love starts, a boot camp for troubled teens, and kids in foster care who might not get to go to a camp otherwise." He reached out and lifted her chin so that she was looking up at him. "No one should have to grow up without a family. This camp can be their family."

Jessica was afraid to ask, but she had to. "Whose camp is this?"

"Mine."

She trembled and swallowed against the thickness in her throat.

Ryan seemed to be waiting for her to say something. When she didn't, he let out a loud sigh and grabbed her hand, hauling her behind him again.

"Good grief, slow down."

He immediately slowed, but kept pulling her along until they reached a clearing with a vast collection of long, rectangular buildings surrounded by wooden fences.

"What's all this?"

"Stables. Next Spring, I'm going to buy twenty head at auction, from my dad, not that he'll know who the buyer is. I'll purchase them anonymously, of course. When the camp opens, each pair of kids will be assigned one horse to take care of. They won't eat until the horse eats. They won't bathe until their horse has been groomed and settled in for the night. They'll learn to care for another living being, and to work as a team to get the work done."

He continued to talk about his plans as he led the way back to the main hall. The whole time they were walking, Jessica's mind was racing with all kinds of crazy thoughts. There was only one reason she could think of for Ryan to buy those horses without letting his father know who'd bought them. And that reason didn't fit with what Ryan had told her the last time she'd seen him.

"This is where my expertise ends," Ryan said, when he led her into the kitchen. "I know you aren't fond of cooking. That's not a problem. I'll hire someone to—"

"Stop it, just stop it." She tugged her hand out of his grasp and stepped back. "Why are you doing this?"

He closed the distance between them. "I've missed you so much, Jessie."

"Don't you dare call me that. You gave up that right weeks ago."

A flash of pain crossed his face. "I never meant to hurt you."

She ducked under his outstretched arms. "Stop it. You're just making everything worse. You're breaking my heart."

"How am I breaking your heart?" He followed her across the kitchen.

She backed away from him. "You're confusing me, you're…you're confusing me."

He kept coming toward her. "I love you, Jessica."

She shook her head. "No, you don't. You love your family. You said you'd never give them up, for anyone. And you shouldn't have to."

He stopped in front of her, but he didn't reach for her. "Do you know what I did after I left you?"

"I don't care."

"I went back home, to my parents' ranch. To forget you."

Hot tears splashed down Jessica's cheeks. Now this was what she'd expected. He was going to hurt her again, after all.

"You're not that easy to forget, Jessie. I was with my family, but the most important part of me was missing. You."

She blinked and stared at him warily. "What are you saying?"

He reached out and caught one of her tears on his finger, then pressed his hand to his heart. "That's the last tear I ever want you to shed because of me, unless you shed happy tears. I've made my peace with my family. We've said our goodbyes, and they've all given me their blessing. I love my family. I'll always love them, but I know now that there's more than one kind of family. The family you're born into, and the family you choose." He tipped her chin up and stared into her eyes. "I choose you."

She jerked away. "No, I don't want you to make that kind of sacrifice for me. You'll only grow to resent me and hate me down the road. And what about your career? What about your family traditions? You can't give all that up, not for me."

"Why not?" His voice had turned angry. "Because you don't think you're worth the sacrifice?"

She glanced away.

He swore and leaned down, forcing her to look at him. "Don't ever say something like that to me again. You are more precious to me than anyone else in the world. No person, no job, could ever mean more to me than you. Do you love me?"

Her heart squeezed in her chest. "You're changing the subject."

"No, I'm trying to solve a problem. I want you. I love you. I want to be with you. I have to know what I'm up against. Do. You. Love. Me?"

"Love isn't the problem, Ryan." At his exasperated look, she said, "Yes. Yes, I love you."

His face smoothed out and he visibly relaxed.

"I don't think you understand," she said. "I love you, but it doesn't matter—"

"You don't think I'd be happy running a boot camp for troubled kids?"

"No, I don't."

"Don't you remember me telling you about the horse camps my family runs every summer? Come on, let me show you something." He tried to grab her hand, but she yanked it back.

"You are not going to drag me somewhere again. You're far too bossy."

His lips twitched. "I'll have to work on that. After you." He waved his hand toward the stairs for her to precede him.

She straightened her spine and headed up the stairs, even though she knew there wasn't any point. He swept past her and opened a door at the end of the hall, politely waiting for her to enter.

It was a large office, with three plain wooden desks, with file cabinets and boxes of varying sizes stacked around the room. He watched her intently, but she wasn't sure exactly what he wanted her to see.

"I don't understand. What do you want to show me?"

"Look at the desks. What do you see?"

She stepped to the nearest desk. The entire surface was covered with photographs. "Pictures, tons of pictures."

He shook his head. "You're not making this easy. Look closely at the pictures."

They were pictures of kids riding horses, mucking out stalls, doing target practice. One of the young teenaged boys caught her attention—a boy with short dark hair, and eyes so blue they were almost black. Ryan. He was helping one of the children get up on a horse. The look of joy on his face was palpable, even in an old photograph.

"Look at these," Ryan said, pointing to another desk.

Jessica crossed, stood beside him and tears flowed down her face again when she saw Ryan working with the children.

"Does that look like a man who's miserable?" he asked.

She shook her head. "No. You look…happy." She traced her finger across his smiling face, then over to another picture. The man and woman smiling back at her had the same blue eyes as Ryan.

"My mom and dad," Ryan said. "My brothers—" he pointed to another picture "—and my sister." He reached out and gently wiped the tears from Jessica's cheeks. "You haven't made me give up my dreams. I told my family all about you. They love you as much as I do because they see how much I love you, and they know you'll make me happy. Those pictures, the ones where they're smiling, were taken *after* I told them I was going into Wit-Sec to spend the rest of my life with you. They're happy for me, for us."

He gently took Jessica's hand and pressed it against his heart. "My family will always be with me, in here. But you're my family now."

A sob escaped Jessica. She squeezed her eyes shut and clenched her fist against her mouth.

"Open your eyes, Jessie." He pressed a soft kiss on the tip of her nose, her eyelashes, the top of her head. "Please," he whispered.

Jessica opened her eyes and blinked up at him through her tears.

Ryan gently brushed her hair out of her face. "I love you, Jessie. I'll never abandon you. If I leave, I'll always come back. Got that?"

Her lower lip trembled and she squeezed her eyes shut again. She shook her head back and forth.

"Tell me there's hope, that there's a future for us," Ryan whispered.

She trembled and opened her eyes. She fisted her hand, drew it back, and punched him in the arm.

His brows shot up in surprise. "Jessie?"

"Rule number one," she said. "If you ever, ever leave me again, I'll take that gun you're so fond of shoving at me and use it for its intended purpose. Got that?"

Ryan narrowed his eyes at her. "You're making fun of me, aren't you, sugar?"

Jessica's lips curved up, smiling for the first time since that terrible night when Ryan had walked out of her life. "Wouldn't dream of it. Shut up and kiss me, Ryan."

He laughed just before his lips touched hers.

Epilogue

Ryan took full advantage of his newfound bribery skills to gain one last favor from WitSec. The Justice Department granted him permission for a reunion with his family, for a very special occasion.

With a heavy contingent of U.S. Marshals surrounding them, Ryan and Jessica were married in Colorado on the Jackson family ranch.

On a horse.

Not each of them on separate horses, as originally planned.

On one horse, together, with Ryan holding Jessica tightly around the waist.

Because Jessica had discovered she was scared to death of horses.

Ryan thought that was hilarious. He couldn't stop laughing until she called him "Elvis."

Then his eyes went dark and he chased her around the barn, demanding to know who had told her his middle name.

If he could keep a secret, so could she. And since she had so much fun when he caught her, she planned on keeping this secret for a very long time.

* * * * *

ReaderService.com

Manage your account online!
- Review your order history
- Manage your payments
- Update your address

---

*We've designed
the Harlequin® Reader Service
website just for you.*

Enjoy all the features!
- Reader excerpts from any series
- Respond to mailings and
  special monthly offers
- Discover new series available to you
- Browse the Bonus Bucks catalog
- Share your feedback

Visit us at:

ReaderService.com

REQUEST YOUR FREE BOOKS!

2 FREE NOVELS
PLUS 2 FREE GIFTS!

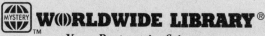

Your Partner in Crime

YES! Please send me 2 FREE novels from the Worldwide Library® series and my 2 FREE gifts (gifts are worth about $10). After receiving them, if I don't wish to receive any more books, I can return the shipping statement marked "cancel." If I don't cancel, I will receive 4 brand-new novels every month and be billed just $5.24 per book in the U.S. or $6.24 per book in Canada. That's a savings of at least 34% off the cover price. It's quite a bargain! Shipping and handling is just 50¢ per book in the U.S. and 75¢ per book in Canada.* I understand that accepting the 2 free books and gifts places me under no obligation to buy anything. I can always return a shipment and cancel at any time. Even if I never buy another book, the two free books and gifts are mine to keep forever.

414/424 WDN FVUV

Name	(PLEASE PRINT)

Address	Apt. #

City	State/Prov.	Zip/Postal Code

Signature (if under 18, a parent or guardian must sign)

Mail to the Harlequin® Reader Service:
IN U.S.A.: P.O. Box 1867, Buffalo, NY 14240-1867
IN CANADA: P.O. Box 609, Fort Erie, Ontario L2A 5X3

Want to try two free books from another line?
Call 1-800-873-8635 or visit www.ReaderService.com.

* Terms and prices subject to change without notice. Prices do not include applicable taxes. Sales tax applicable in N.Y. Canadian residents will be charged applicable taxes. Offer not valid in Quebec. This offer is limited to one order per household. Not valid for current subscribers to the Worldwide Library series. All orders subject to credit approval. Credit or debit balances in a customer's account(s) may be offset by any other outstanding balance owed by or to the customer. Please allow 4 to 6 weeks for delivery. Offer available while quantities last.

Your Privacy—The Harlequin® Reader Service is committed to protecting your privacy. Our Privacy Policy is available online at www.ReaderService.com or upon request from the Harlequin Reader Service.

We make a portion of our mailing list available to reputable third parties that offer products we believe may interest you. If you prefer that we not exchange your name with third parties, or if you wish to clarify or modify your communication preferences, please visit us at www.ReaderService.com/consumerschoice or write to us at Harlequin Reader Service Preference Service, P.O. Box 9062, Buffalo, NY 14269. Include your complete name and address.

WWLI3